CIRCLE OF DECEIT

An Interracial Romance

KASEY MARTIN

D1564248

Jessica Watkins Presents

PROLOGUE

PAST INDISCRETIONS

The sun was shining, and the breeze was gentle as he sat at an outdoor café in Dallas, Texas. The beautiful fall day was just what he needed to take his mind off of his growing problems.

Then he saw her, one of the most striking women to ever cross his path. His eyes roamed hungrily over her willowy frame. Every seductive sway of her hips made his mouth water. She was walking temptation and just the type of distraction he needed.

He had had many women in his life; blonds, brunettes, white, black, it didn't matter to him. But this woman was a breath of fresh air, and he could tell she was different than the rest.

Her hair whipped in the wind causing the tresses to fall into her sparkling green eyes. When she paused and smiled at him, he knew it was love at first sight.

Nothing would keep him away from this gorgeous being who ensnared him with a single glance. And it must've been his lucky day because she didn't continue on her way like he suspected she would. No, she walked right up to the small outdoor table and smiled mischievously.

Her sweet perfume enchanted and reminded him of the things he longed for and of the things he desperately wanted again. He couldn't help the wolfish grin that covered his face.

"I'm Alexander." He held out his hand, and when her small delicate fingers caressed his, the sparks began to fly.

❧ I ❧

SOMETHING NEW

She felt the calloused hand as it glided roughly over her sensitive nipples, tweaking and twisting the delicate buds until they hardened in pleasure. The butterflies in her belly were fluttering wildly, and her breathing was becoming more and more erratic with every teasing touch of his masterful fingers.

His digits slipped from her nipples and down over her belly and oh so close to the apex of her thighs. She tensed in anticipation, wanting and needing to feel his fingers on her swelling core, but his sweet, sweet touch disappeared leaving her breathless once again.

"Please, I need more. Just touch me. Please!" she begged? in a voice ragged with lust. She'd never begged before, but today she was shameless.

"Shhhh. No begging. You know the rules. I'll give you what you need." His voice was deep with a hint of darkness that made her body shiver and her core pulsate.

Never in a million years would Raquel Vincent, a counselor from Small Town, USA, have ever thought that she, of all people, would be in this situation. Her naked body was splayed open, her hands and legs were secured to the bed tightly with silk ties while her vision was obscured by a blindfold.

Because of the darkness, Raquel's senses were on high alert. Her heart raced, pulse pounded loudly in her ears, and best of all, she felt every delicious touch of the masculine hand playing her body like an instrument. Her pussy ached in anticipation. It clenched in and out, waiting to be filled. Although the excitement she felt was undeniable, the guilt sizzled just beneath the surface. However, she knew what she'd signed up for; she agreed to go do this.

All of this was new for Raquel; being vocal in the bedroom, lustfully begging, and definitely being tied to a bed. She wasn't at all adventurous, especially in the bedroom. However, in the last year, she and her husband, Alexander, had been trying new things to spice up their nearly twelve-year marriage. He had convinced her that letting go and having fun sexually wasn't a bad thing, and as a married couple, they needed to try new things.

However, being dominated hadn't ever crossed her mind as the spice they needed. She had never fantasized about such things. Her and Alexander's sex life was the definition of vanilla. Now, Raquel wasn't a prude or even uptight about sex. She just considered herself traditional, so she had to give credit to her husband for pushing her beyond her boundaries. She had always been a safe missionary position with a little doggy style thrown in from time to time kind of girl, and she'd never considered herself a sex kitten. To be completely honest, Raquel didn't actually think about her sexuality.

The feel of his wet tongue licking its way down the valley of her breasts brought her out of her thoughts and back to her current predicament. Her back arched off the bed, and her moan was torturously low. Raquel pulled at her restraints trying to get closer to his mouth when he once again pulled it away from her. She huffed in frustration at his teasing chuckle.

"Now, now, you're so eager. I've already tied your hands and legs, but you still insist on trying to move that delectable body to entice me." He tsked, and even though Raquel couldn't see his gorgeous face, she knew that a smirk covered those tempting kissable lips of his.

"You said you would give me what I wanted." She could hear the whine in her voice, but she couldn't help herself. The hot flames of her desire were burning her from the inside out.

"No. I said I would give you what you *needed*." Raquel could hear the amusement in his voice, and if she weren't so horny, she would've been embarrassed by how out of control she was acting. But she couldn't seem to stop herself.

"What I need is your mouth on my pussy," she boldly growled as she tilted her pelvis up off the bed. She shocked herself with the naughty words that flowed from her mouth, but tonight, she was a wanton woman.

The dip in the bed and the heat from his body hovered over her, and it made Raquel giddy. She knew it was only a matter of time before his mouth would greedily lap at her core.

"Ummm, your pretty slit is already leaking for me." Raquel felt his thick finger slide up and down her core. She stifled her moan, afraid he would take away the pleasure.

"Oh, no you don't!" he growled low as he thrust his thick digit inside of her. "You think you can keep your moans from me?" He pumped faster until she couldn't hold in the shout of ecstasy that was followed by a full body shiver.

"I earned these moans. You give me my shit!" His harsh words in her ear made Raquel regret that she ever tried to hold back her pleasure from the beast still hovering over her.

"I-I won't do it again. Please..." She trailed off, unable to finish because of the overwhelming feeling of excitement coursing through her veins.

Raquel didn't know which way was up. Her body was set ablaze from his manipulations. Again, the thought of how she'd gotten here ran through her mind. She never thought she would be the kind of woman who would be burning up from a man's touch.

BUT THIS, THIS MAN RUBBING ON HER NIPPLES AND PUSSY AS IF HE owned them. Making her body sing in ways that she couldn't imagine. It made her acutely aware of not only her sexuality but her sensuality as well.

"Please take the blindfold off. I just want to see. Please." Raquel was so out of her depth. She had no idea how to handle all of her senses being out of whack.

"No." His voice reverberated in her ear.

"You know the rules, Rocky. And I won't remind you again."

"That's funny. You didn't seem like the rule following type," Raquel pushed to get her way, which was out of the ordinary for her.

He grunted his displeasure at her defiant words. He stopped moving his fingers, and it was Raquel's turn to grunt out her frustrations.

"You didn't seem like the talkative type, yet here we are." She could hear the smile in his voice, and it made her wish that she could actually move to get her way.

"Maybe I should put that sweet little hole to better use? Maybe if I filled your mouth with cock, you wouldn't have so much to say?" His voice was low and animalistic.

"Maybe." The one word was flippant, but her insides quivered at the thought of his glorious cock in her mouth.

"Hmm..." he hummed before she felt his body lift off of hers. His movements were swift and silent. And no matter how hard she tried to listen, she couldn't tell where he was in the room.

Then his breath suddenly warmed her ear as he spoke, "You're a beautiful, sexy woman, Rocky. But you're trying to dominate as a submissive. Now that's not what we agreed on. You wanted to be dominated, to give up control. If you weren't ready for my style of play, then you shouldn't have chosen me."

His words were a warning for her to follow the rules, the rules that she agreed to before their tryst, and she tried to let go and be free just like her husband was doing. But she just couldn't get out of her own head.

"Okay. You're right. I'm sorry," Raquel apologized after taking a deep breath.

"That's my good girl. Now I'm going to eat your sweet pussy until you cum down my throat and then I'm going to fill every one of your sweet holes with my cock. And you're going to scream my name while I do it."

"Y-Yes." Raquel stammered.

"Yes, what?" he questioned darkly, his rough hands once again rubbing slow circles over her nipples.

"Yes, sir," she conceded on a sigh when she felt his hot mouth against her center.

"Ummm, you taste just like I imagined you would." Her thighs muffled his words, but she could still hear the lust dripping from every syllable he uttered.

His tongue flicked at her clit until it was swollen with desire. He sucked her lower lips into his mouth, as he licked up and down her slit like it was the best ice cream sundae he had ever tasted. His hands still played with her nipples as he brought her to the precipice of pleasure.

Raquel wanted to beg him not to stop, but that would be breaking the rules. She was supposed to take any and everything that he gave her or he would stop. She was submissive in this scenario, and he was dominant. It's what she asked for. It's what she thought she could handle.

Raquel squirmed, wishing not for the first time that she wasn't tied up. She wanted to feel the full experience and getting her hands on his hard muscular body was the ultimate goal.

"I'm going to untie your legs because I want you to wrap them around my waist when I'm deep inside you."

Raquel smiled. It wasn't her hands, but she would take what she could get.

He untied her ankles and rubbed his hands up and down her thighs before he slipped into her heated pussy with ease. Raquel sighed at the sensual invasion. His kiss upon her lips was next, and as she tasted herself on his wet tongue, her lust ramped up to an all-time high.

His thrusts were deep with a steady pace that had her legs quivering around his waist. Chill bumps had broken out all over her body, and her heart thumped wildly in her chest.

"You're going to scream my name, sweet Rocky," he said, breathing raggedly and speeding up his pace like a madman.

He was definitely on a mission, and Raquel couldn't say she was mad at all. His heated cock was moving so thoroughly inside her sugary walls that she didn't realize that her small breathless gasps had grown into loud wails of pleasure.

She had never in all of her life felt so out of control, so methodically worked over. It made her feel a little guilty for screaming his name like a prayer.

"Noah! Noah, oh my gawd! Oh shit, I'm going to cum!" Raquel tensed and then with one final thrust, her world shattered. Her body shook, and tears fell from her eyes and slipped from beneath the blindfold unchecked.

"Say my name, baby! Say. My. Mother. Fucking. Name," he punctuated each word with a hard thrust, and Raquel's resolve to feel guilty was weakened with every achingly satisfyingly penetrating plunge of his manhood.

"Nooooaaaah!" she moaned loudly as she came once more. She felt Noah stiffen before she felt the ripples of his ecstasy through the latex that separated them.

"Oh, fuck! Raquel, your pussy..." He didn't finish his words as his massive body collapsed on her.

His damp hair tickled the side of her face as he nuzzled her neck before he lifted up and released her from her binds. He slipped the blindfold from her eyes, and she smiled.

"You okay?" His ocean blue eyes searched hers sincerely, and it made her grateful that he was such a gentleman.

"I'm fine. I'm more than fine, actually, I'm great." She couldn't believe she had done it. After twelve years of marriage and fifteen years together, Raquel had slept with someone other than her husband.

"I know this is your first time doing all of this, but I promise it doesn't have to be awkward. We're friends that shared something special, and believe me, your husband wouldn't want you to feel guilty." Noah's words were heartfelt, and she trusted him. After all, he and his wife were pros at this game. She and her husband were the newbies in this situation.

"I wouldn't have done this with you if I thought it would be awkward," Raquel responded thoughtfully.

"Good. I'm glad you trust me. Now, let's take a shower and go back to the party. I'm sure my wife and your husband will be back already." Noah smiled at her with his twinkling eyes and dimples, and she melted just a little inside.

"Thank you for making me feel so comfortable. I would've never been able to go through with this if it weren't for your patience." Raquel had been reluctant to participate in the swinger's lifestyle, but her husband, Alexander, had wanted to try it.

Alexander had brought up the subject casually, and Raquel had been devastated. She thought that after so many years together her husband had grown tired of her and instead of cheating outright, he wanted her to be involved in some hedonistic mess.

She cried, wondering if at thirty-seven she would be getting a divorce and having to start over. However, her husband had convinced her that she wasn't unattractive to him and he still loved her with all his heart. He just wanted to spice things up and be upfront about it. Alexander told her he had made a mistake, and he regretted hurting her.

Raquel felt Alexander's words were genuine and he never pushed her. So, after a lot of research and questions, Raquel was curious enough to try swinging for the first time. She felt she owed it to her husband to at least look into what he wanted. So she did, and their journey of lust had begun.

❧ 2 ❧

UNEXPECTED INFATUATIONS

Noah washed Raquel's body thoroughly. His hands replaced the loofa as they slid along her slick body. He massaged the tension from her neck and shoulders as he tried with all his might to control the hard-on that threatened to spring to life at the view and feel of all her tasty curves.

When Noah first saw Raquel, he couldn't help but notice how beautiful she was. She stood tall for a woman at around five feet nine. Her legs were so long they seemed to go on for miles. He imagined the silky brown limbs wrapped around his head, and his heartbeat spiked. It was an instant attraction, but it wasn't unusual for Noah to be attracted to a beautiful woman. He was a red-blooded male with a healthy sexual appetite. But what was unexpected was for him to notice all the minute details of this virtual stranger.

Noah continued to caress her curves, no longer washing her body as Raquel stepped completely under the flow of water, letting the water cascade over her short, cropped hair. Noah was surprised because he had been with black women before and he knew that getting their hair wet was a definite no-no.

When she turned around, her deep dark eyes that reminded him of onyx twinkled with mirth. "Our vigorous activities sweated my hair out, so I need to let the natural curls come out, or I'm going to look a hot mess for the rest of the night." She shrugged with a little laugh in explanation that he found endearing.

Noah laughed. "Hey, I've been around the block a time or two and I know that you don't mess with a black woman's hair."

They shared a laugh, and he could tell that Raquel relaxed a little more. Noah knew from experience that after the lust haze had worn off and reality kicked in, some people would allow shame to overtake them and it could become awkward quickly. However, he didn't feel like anyone should feel ashamed of owning their sexuality.

In Noah's opinion, people were entirely too uptight and needed to let loose and be free. People worried too much about what other's thought of them instead of being happy. As long as you weren't hurting anyone else, he didn't see the harm in engaging in sex with whomever you wished. He believed what he and his wife were involved in was nobody's business but theirs.

People stood on their moral high ground looking down their noses at others who they deemed to be beneath them, but Noah didn't give a fuck about those people. He loved his wife, and she loved him. Sex was just that, sex. It was an activity that they did with one another and sometimes, other people. Their love for each other wasn't based upon their sexual relationships.

"Hey, you okay?" Raquel's sweet voice filled his ears, and he smiled down at her.

"Yeah, I'm good. We better get out and head down to the party." The words tasted like acid on his tongue. The last thing he wanted to do was leave her, which was a problem. He was never this infatuated with a woman before.

When he first met Raquel and her husband, Alexander, he could smell the naïveté pouring from them. He hated dealing with newbies. The swinging lifestyle wasn't for everyone because sometimes people confused lust with love and those situations could turn messy fast. So he and his wife liked to engage with people who were familiar with how things worked, and they usually stayed far away from the "explorers" of the culture.

Noah wasn't an expert on all things swinging, but he and his wife had lived the life for the past seven years, and he'd made his mistakes in the past. That's why there were rules in place. And they were rules he typically followed without deviation.

However, after some very hot convincing from his extremely sensual wife, Giselle, he decided why the hell not.

Giselle's narrow hips swayed seductively as she moved gracefully in Noah's direction. She licked her plumped red painted lips, and straddled his lap. Noah wasn't sure what he'd done to deserve such a treat from his wife, but he wasn't going to ask too many questions.

Giselle ran her nails down Noah's chest as she graced him with a sultry smile. "There was something I wanted to ask you. And you can say no, but I really hope you'll like my idea."

Noah's interest was piqued. "What's up?"

Giselle kissed and sucked on his neck, then she made her way to her knees. "There's a couple here at the resort. They look a little lost, so maybe we can show them where to find a good time?" Noah intently watched her as she slowly pulled down his zipper.

Her long blond hair obscured his view, so he wrapped it in his fist as she began to convince him that a novice couple was worth their time.

That was his first mistake. Now he was standing in a shower wondering how he could spend more time with a woman he'd only met a week and a half ago.

Noah shook his head, his slightly long blond hair moving with the motion. He turned off the water and exited the shower. He grabbed the fluffy white towel and passed it to Raquel before grabbing one for himself.

They slowly dried themselves, stealing heated lustful looks at one another. His body instantly reacted to the desire reflected in the dark pools of her eyes. Noah took a deep breath, relenting to the fact that as long as Raquel was in his presence, he would be in a state of perpetual hardness.

"You know if you keep looking at me like that, I just might have to get you all dirty again." Noah smirked and when Raquel bit her plump bottom berry colored lip, he groaned.

Before he could use common sense, Noah pulled her into his arms and kissed her with all the passion he felt coursing through his veins.

His teeth replaced hers, biting into her bottom lip. He licked away the pain and continued to devour her mouth.

She tasted sweet like the strawberries and champagne they had earlier. He also tasted her nervousness. He couldn't imagine why she would still be nervous after all they had done.

He reluctantly pulled away from her luscious lips and looked deeply into her eyes trying to find the cause of her worries, but she quickly turned away from his intense stare.

"We should get dressed." Raquel turned away from him and gathered her dress that was thrown over the chair. He watched as she gracefully slipped it over her head.

The purple material glided over her curves like liquid. She sat down and slid her feet into the matching high heeled stilettos. She stood and ran her hands down her body, straightening out her dress. Noah could only stare mesmerized by her every movement like a teenaged boy with his first crush.

He sighed to himself as he began to dress. It was an unexpected infatuation. And although this was the first time for him to feel this way, Noah knew he would get over it. Eventually.

As they re-entered the room full of partygoers, Noah could see the tension returning to Raquel's posture. Her stance was stiff and rigid. His hand tightened around hers in reassurance.

Although they had just had mind blowing out of this world sex, he still didn't know the woman standing beside him very well. But Noah could tell she was uncomfortable. It was her first time at the erotic resort. Diamond's was a resort that specialized in the swinging lifestyle. It was a place that couples could go without fear of judgment and spend a tropical vacation with like-minded individuals.

A friend of Giselle's had recommended the resort, and they had been coming at least twice a year for the past four years. The place was luxurious and relaxing. It was a no pressure environment, and if you decided not to engage in the activities that were offered it wasn't an issue.

Although a lot of couples participated, there were some that leaned more to the voyeuristic side and only watched. It didn't bother him what others chose to do. Everyone had their kinks.

"I don't see Alexander and Giselle. Do you think they're still..." Raquel's words trailed off and her dark eyes were worry filled. She turned away in embarrassment, but not before Noah caught the distressed look on her beautiful oval shaped face.

"Listen, there isn't any reason you need to be concerned. I'm sure Alexander and Giselle are just enjoying themselves." Noah placed his hand softly under Raquel's chin and turned her face toward him. "Let's get a drink and relax, so you can stop fretting over things that are already done."

Noah wrapped his arm around her waist and squeezed her before leading her to the bar. It was something about Raquel that made him want to shelter her. Although he could see she was a strong-willed individual, the vulnerability that she displayed caused all of his protective instincts to kick in.

After receiving two strong cocktails from the bar, Noah found a quaint table in the corner with a view of the room. Raquel was fidgeting and searching around the room every few seconds until Noah grabbed her hands, forcing her hold still. The stress was rolling off of her in waves.

"Tell me what's really going on with you. And I want the truth." Noah's voice held an edge to it that he didn't often display. Something was going on with the beautiful woman sitting across from him, and he wanted to know what it was.

Raquel sighed heavily before twisting her wedding band around her slender finger. "I-I didn't want to do this."

Noah lifted his brows, but not out of shock. Anyone could see that Raquel was out of her depth. She looked as if she could make a diamond if she sat on a piece of coal. From the time she'd stepped foot on the resort, her demeanor had been uptight and weary. Tonight had been the exception when he finally got her to relax. But Noah suspected that the sex and role playing had a lot to do with that.

"You don't say." Noah tried to hide his chuckle, but from the way Raquel pursed her lips, he knew she'd heard him.

"I'm glad you can make light of this situation, but this is my life." She huffed.

Noah felt bad when he saw the glassy sheen in her beautiful eyes. "Hey, there's no need for tears." Noah scooted his chair close to hers, so he could wrap his arm around her shoulders.

"I just don't know what the hell I'm doing anymore. I can't believe I slept with you."

Noah frowned. He knew for certain he was good in bed, and from the way that she was screaming his name and moaning the place down; she definitely enjoyed it.

Noah leaned back in his chair as he assessed the woman next to him. He was so full of lust before he hadn't noticed that Raquel was obviously hiding something.

"So, why did you choose to sleep with me if it wasn't what you wanted?"

"It was what my husband wanted. He's the one who chose you, not me."

Noah's eyes widened at Raquel's admission. He never once suspected Alexander had made such a big decision for his wife. At the Diamonds Resort, the woman always chose her partner. It assured there weren't any misunderstandings or accusations. If Alexander chose for Raquel, then they had broken a major rule of not only the resort but the lifestyle.

"I know you all are new to this, but you sure as hell know that's not how this shit works." Noah was pissed. He made sure that he went over every minute detail of the rules with Raquel before their night began. He spent time with her to make sure she was comfortable, and she never once mentioned that she wasn't a willing participant.

"I'm not going to accuse you of anything, Noah. So you have nothing to worry about. I did this to save my marriage. And Alexander felt comfortable with you."

"Sweetheart, I hate to tell you, but swingin' aint gonna save your marriage. Spice it up, maybe. Open it up, definitely. But save it, not a chance in hell."

"You don't know anything about me, Noah!" Raquel's voice was shrill.

"I know what you've told me, which by the way, seems to be a load of bullshit," Noah responded calmly.

"I tried my best to go with the flow, but this isn't how I saw my marriage going." She paused and when she looked up at Noah the tears were back. "I just wanted my husband to be happy."

"Darlin', if a man asks you to do something you're uncomfortable with and he knows you're against it, his happiness is detrimental to your well-being," Noah responded seriously.

"We've been together fifteen years. He's all I know."

"Well, it's about time you get to know yourself. Don't you think?" Noah leaned over and caught her falling tears with his thumb. "I know you didn't choose me, but I thought we were getting to know each other a little. I make a helluva friend."

Raquel smiled weakly. "Thanks, but this whole thing was a mistake. I just need my husband to get here, so we can leave."

Noah leaned over, steepling his hands on top of the table. He had been patient with the woman up until now. But if she wanted to act like she didn't know what the real deal was then he would give her a reality check.

"What's done is done, darlin'. You're on a tropical island paradise with a bunch of people who just want to fuck, drink, and relax in that order. So, you might as well join the fun. Because your husband sure as fuck won't be ready to leave, and you can bet your pretty ass on that."

He watched Raquel take a deep breath, but the tears were still in her eyes. Noah knew that he shouldn't have taken a chance on a novice couple. But like he said to Raquel, what's done is done and there was no turning back.

✻ 3 ✻

TRUE LIES

Raquel was disappointed. She trusted Noah, and he had been all sunshine and rainbows until she dropped her panties. Then, just like the typical man, his attitude changed with the wind. It was true she and Alexander had broken the rules of Diamond's Resort, but it wasn't to hurt Noah or Giselle.

"I'm not sure if I can do this, Alexander. I mean can't we just be voyeurs?" Raquel anxiously bit her nails while bouncing her legs up and down.

"Raquel, we've gone over this. You agreed." Alexander's stern voice brokered no argument.

"But what if I don't find anyone that I like? Am I supposed to sit back and watch you with another woman while by myself?" She tried and failed to keep the panic out of her voice.

Alexander sighed loudly, before rubbing his temples slowly.

His exasperation with her questions were written all over his face, however, it didn't curve Raquel's nervousness. Normally, she would stop aggravating him with all of her apprehension, but it was at an all-time high since she stepped foot onto the resort.

"Just relax, okay? You don't have to pick a man. I met a very nice woman in the lobby named, Giselle. She and her husband are going to show us the ropes."

Alexander sounded relaxed about the whole thing, and Raquel wished she could have the same go with the flow attitude.

She let Alexander choose her partner because she didn't have the nerve to pick a man to sleep with after only knowing him a week. It was entirely out of her character to even think of such a thing. It didn't matter *who* the man was because she only wanted to make her husband happy. She just wanted to go back to being the loving couple they'd been in the past. She had no plans to continue this lifestyle after this vacation.

Alexander had promised her if she tried this for him, they could try to finally start a family. He convinced her that all he wanted was a little excitement before they became parents, so she agreed.

Raquel had been pushing Alexander for a family for years. She'd met him when she was twenty-two and fresh out of college. Although he wasn't her first boyfriend, he definitely was her first love and the only man she had ever made love to. All she ever wanted was a family, and to be loved by her husband. She just wanted to please him and make him happy, but she knew deep down this wasn't the way to do it. She had pushed her morals to the side in order to get her way, and she just hoped that her marriage could survive it.

However, it felt like she had thrown away their love, the vows they recited to one another to be faithful, and the trust they once shared. It didn't matter that she had agreed to come to the resort, and to sleep with someone else. It didn't matter that Alexander knew and it was his idea. All that mattered was the deep feeling of guilt Raquel couldn't seem to shake.

The guilt was potent, specifically when she looked at Noah. Raquel had never been so wanton with Alexander. She'd never begged or pleaded or even used foul language in bed. She was the definition of a prim and proper wife. But tonight, she had acted like a lustful slut with no self-control and she was ashamed of herself.

"Listen, I get that you're in some kind of turmoil for whatever reason and I'm only trying to be real about what goes on here. Whether you like it or not, your husband is here for the full experience. So you might as well just relax." Noah's voice broke the uncomfortable silence.

"Thank you for your advice, Noah," Raquel snapped. If he told her to relax one more freaking time she was going to lose her shit.

How could she relax when her husband was off with another woman having the time of his life according to Noah? She knew how excited Alexander was to be here. Hell, it was all he could talk about for weeks. Raquel had to get tipsy off champagne just to go to the room with Noah, and now that it was all said and done she couldn't help but wonder about her husband. *What if Giselle was a better lover? What if Alexander wanted to continue swinging? What if he wanted a divorce?* Raquel's thoughts were starting to spiral and she was going to have a panic attack if she didn't regain control.

"Hey, there's no need to get snippy. I'm just trying to help you. I've been new to this and I know what you're going through, but stressing out about it isn't going to help." Noah nonchalantly shrugged his broad shoulders before he sipped his bourbon.

Raquel envied how calm and collected he was. But there was no emotion under his cool façade, and it bothered her. Was he so desensitized? Did it really not bother him that his wife was screwing another man? Was it really just sex?

Raquel's arched brow raised in disapproval. "Telling me not to stress is the same as telling me to relax. Neither are helpful."

Noah smirked, his right dimple peeking out on his handsome face. He swept his blond hair out of his face, and his blue eyes twinkled in her direction. It was as if he were a professional at seducing women. Hell, maybe he was. Raquel fell for him hook, line, and sinker after only a week of knowing him.

"Just trying to help, Rocky. I know what you're going through. That's all I'm trying to say." He smiled sincerely, and although she kept her face carefully blank, her resolve to be mad melted a little.

Raquel wanted to continue to be salty with Noah and his easy going attitude. She wanted to blame him for the guilt she was feeling. She didn't want to feel the lustful swoon that was trying to bubble up at his cute little nickname or his beautiful smile. He made her feel things that Alexander never took the time to even care about.

"Where did you get this 'Rocky' stuff from anyway? Nobody has ever called me that in my life." Raquel tried to keep her smile at bay, but no matter what she did, she couldn't suppress it.

"What? You don't like it?" Noah asked, still smiling.

Raquel shrugged. She didn't want to give away the fact that it made her feel special. She especially didn't want to seem like an inexperienced adolescent with a crush. She wanted to be mad, but she wasn't. Noah was the only good thing about this whole experience.

She wanted to hold his crass words against him, but he had every right to be upset about Alexander choosing him. It was the second major rule at Diamond's that ladies choose. The first rule was that all swinging couples wore black rings to signify they were willing participants.

At the thought of the black ring she twisted it around her right ring finger. It would always be a physical reminder of what she had done. Raquel wanted to take it off and throw it in the nearest garbage bin. But, that was against the rules. The ring stayed on until you left the resort.

As her blood pressure began to spike with shame, she saw her husband walk into the room. At five-foot-eleven, he was only a few inches taller than she was, but he carried himself like a seven-foot giant. He walked with swagger and confidence that attracted Raquel from the jump. She began to smile until she saw the way Alexander was looking at the petite blond standing beside him. His brown eyes were lit up, and his tan face was flushed with the "I just got laid" look.

Raquel watched as Alexander gave his full attention to Giselle. He caressed her face lovingly, and tucked her silky hair behind her ear as he stared into her big green eyes. When he leaned down and kissed her lips with a passion Raquel hadn't seen in years, she turned away. She could no longer watch her husband fawn over another woman. No matter what she agreed to, this shit was not it!

"I'm such a fool." Raquel shook her head as she narrowed her almond shaped eyes at her husband.

RAQUEL HAD DRUNK MORE THAN SHE'D ANTICIPATED TRYING TO

calm her nerves and now she was full on wasted. She sat at the bar with several shots lined up as she tried to drown her sorrows at the bottom of a shot glass. She angrily watched Alexander as he continued to dance and romance Giselle like they were on a fucking honeymoon.

When Alexander had the audacity to smile and wave at her from the dance floor, Raquel gulped down more liquor to numb the pain. He didn't even give her enough consideration to come and say hello. It was as if the woman on his arm was his wife and Raquel was the stranger. She could feel herself getting angrier by the minute, and even more sad. She had known all along it was a mistake to come here, but she wanted a baby so bad. Raquel had even stopped her birth control to get prepared for their new beginning. But the joke was on her.

She watched from the bar as Alexander pulled Giselle by the waist and ground into her petite bottom. "I always knew he wanted a flat ass chick, I got too much junk in the trunk." Raquel mumbled to herself. When she picked up her fourth shot, the bartender happily replaced it with another.

"Little lady, I suggest you slow down on those shots." Noah took the glass from her hand right as she was about to turn it up.

"Aye-hey I was drinking that." Raquel hiccupped as she sluggishly tried to grab the glass back.

"Nah. I think you've had enough slugger. Let's go outside for some fresh air."

Raquel felt Noah tugging her toward the exit, but she had no control over her body. The cool island breeze hit her as soon as she took a step outside, and she inhaled deeply before tripping on her wobbly legs.

"Whoa! Hell, those dang buttery nipples are starting to kick in." Raquel giggled drunkenly.

"Sweetheart, you stopped drinking buttery nipples an hour ago." Noah chuckled. "You've been downing whiskey for the past forty-five minutes."

"Wait! I was drinking *whiskey*?" Raquel's foggy brain couldn't pull up the memory of her switching to whiskey.

"Yep, Fireball to be exact."

"Awe shit, Fireball gives me amnesia. I never remember anything after drinking whiskey," Raquel moaned as she ran her fingers through her short curls.

She heard Noah's deep rumble of laughter, and it made her laugh. Raquel laughed until tears ran down her cheeks from amusement. Then, as the tears kept flowing and the laughter died down the tears transformed into sadness and heartbreak.

Noah hugged her tightly in comfort, and she hugged him back. Raquel needed to feel the strong arms of a man who wanted her, especially since her husband was living it up with another woman.

"Noah?"

"Yeah, Rocky?"

"Can you take me upstairs, and help me forget just for tonight. Please?"

"Yeah, sweetheart." Noah didn't say anything else as he led her around the outdoor patio and up the back stairs to the suite they'd left earlier.

Raquel was officially drunk, but she could still feel the heartbreak of her husband's rejection. So, she needed the feel of Noah's rough hands against her skin once more to help her forget the sting of dismissal.

Noah pulled her purple dress and her lace panties over her hips and down her long legs. Déjà vu hit Raquel with a vengeance. It was just three hours ago that they were engaging in the same activity. But this time, she didn't want to play a role. She didn't want to be tied up and blindfolded. This time, she wanted to see and feel *everything*.

Noah laid her down on the bed as he undressed. Raquel took the time to marvel at the magnificent man standing in front of her. His rippling muscles made his tattoo's dance. The calloused feel of his palms were in direct contrast to the smooth glow of his sun kissed skin.

Once Noah was completely nude, Raquel sat up on her elbows to get a better view. Although her vision was a little blurry, there was no way she could miss the glorious being standing in front of her.

"You're beautiful," Raquel commented as she absently rubbed her hand down his chiseled chest.

"No. *You're* the beautiful one." Noah kissed her lips sweetly.

He explored her mouth with his slick tongue. Raquel sighed and kissed him back with fierceness she didn't know she was capable of. Noah slid his hand down to her waiting core. He delved his fingers deep within her sweetness, caressing and loving her body with every touch.

Noah rolled over to the bedside table and grabbed a condom. He slipped it on and before the anticipation could build, he pushed into her to the hilt. Noah lifted up on his knees and her legs automatically wrapped around his waist. He pumped in and out at a rapid pace. Her breasts were pressed against his chest and she could feel their hearts beating in tandem. The slippery sound of him moving inside of her wet channel made her hotter than she'd ever been in her life.

"Yes, fuck me!" Raquel screamed uninhibited.

"Do you like this cock? Take this dick baby! Fuck! You feel good," Noah grunted as he moved faster.

Noah slid his fingers between their bodies and found her clit. He rubbed her hot little button until she screamed his name and gushed all over him.

"Yes! That's it baby. Cum on my dick!" Noah demanded as he continued to pump his swollen cock into her tight wet core.

"You feel so good, Noah. Shit!" Raquel purred the words this time without guilt or shame. The alcohol had her beautifully numb, but she wouldn't blame the whiskey. She knew she wanted Noah and she would take everything he gave her.

"This is going to be quick, darlin'. But I promise to make it up to you on the next round." Raquel wouldn't tell him he didn't have to make up anything. He was slinging the best dick she had ever had, so she sure as hell wasn't going to argue with him. If he wanted another round, she was definitely down.

Before she knew it, another orgasm was building. "I'm about to cum again!" Raquel yelled.

"Of course you are, darlin'." Noah growled before he climaxed with her.

🟊 4 🟊

UNGUARDED

I t was the wee hours of the morning when Noah and Raquel sat wrapped in each other's arms, sipping on expensive champagne. The intimacy Noah felt was unusual, and it made him feel on edge. It was never this simple with other lovers. Hell, it wasn't even this easy with his wife. In the past, swinging was about getting a release. It was fun and exciting to have a new partner, but there wasn't any intimacy or whispered secrets. But this was different. Raquel was different.

"You want to know something?" Her sweet voice was thoughtful, and her words gained Noah's full attention.

"I want to know anything you want to tell me, darlin'," Noah responded.

"I cried when Alexander first asked me to swing."

"Really? Why?" Noah genuinely wanted to know, not that he was surprised by her confession.

Raquel snuggled into his chest more as she took a big gulp of the bubbly. "I thought I wasn't enough. I've only ever been with Alexander. Well, before you." She smiled shyly. "I was very young and inexperienced, but over the years I made sure my husband was satisfied. At least, I thought he was satisfied." Raquel sighed heavily.

"Wow." Noah would've never guessed Raquel had only experienced one sexual partner. She was an excellent lover and if she was his, he wasn't sure if he would be able to share her. He shook his head in dismay.

Raquel must've felt the movement because she looked up at him. "I know, right?" She shook her head as she let out a sad chuckle. Noah felt compelled to pull her closer to his body.

He wanted to comfort Raquel as much as possible. But he also wanted to bask in the weight of her against his body for however long they had left. Noah kissed the top of her head and she sighed once more. The sound hardened his cock. It was amazing how one woman could turn his world upside down. From the sound of her sweet voice to the shy way she smiled at him. He was really and truly out of his league with this woman.

"So why did you come here if you didn't want to do this? I know you said you wanted to save your marriage, but it just seems like it's more to it." Noah sipped from his glass as he waited for her to answer. Raquel was a mystery that Noah was all too willing to figure out.

"He promised me a baby," she said simply.

Noah felt a pang in his chest. He wasn't sure why the words hit him so deeply, but the last thing he wanted to do was examine it.

"That's a big promise," he responded after a beat of silence.

"I've always wanted a family, and he used that to his advantage. He's been putting off having kids for years. I just thought he was finally ready, but in hindsight, that was a foolish assumption. Anyone that wants to try swinging isn't ready to start a family."

"That's not always the case. A lot of couples with children are still swingers. One doesn't negate the other." Noah argued.

People had so many stigmas. Just because you had a family, it didn't mean a couple couldn't do what they wanted within their marriage.

"I guess. But I still feel stupid. I should've never agreed to do this, but what's done is done." She smirked up at him and he gave her a lopsided smile.

"Yep, darlin', what's done is done." Noah replied, kissing Raquel on her pillow soft lips.

She kissed him back with so much passion that he instinctively pulled her on top of him. Raquel straddled his hips as her hands moved up and down his muscular chest. Noah couldn't contain the growl that bubbled up from deep within him, so resisting taking over the kiss wasn't even a thought.

"Make me forget, Noah." He could hear the pleading in her voice, but he wouldn't make her beg. Right now wasn't about her submitting. She needed comfort, and he wanted to be there for her even if it was just for the moment.

He obliged her desperate plea as he placed Raquel on her back gently. Noah kissed down her neck and collar bone. He took his time caressing and kissing every erogenous zone he'd found on her body earlier that night.

The little spot on the back of her neck, her sensitive ear lobes, and one of his favorite parts of her succulent body, her breasts.

Her whimpers turned into moans, and Noah delighted in the sound. He pushed into her waiting channel slowly. He wanted to prolong the feeling of her tight pussy wrapped around his cock.

His hips rocked back and forth, picking up speed with each thrust. Noah wanted to help Raquel forget her problems. Hell, he wanted to forget his own. His life wasn't perfect, but his issues weren't as deep as hers.

They made love until the sun came up, and then they just held each other and talked. Noah had to be honest. He didn't want his time with Raquel to end. He found out more about her and he shared some things about himself. He realized they had a lot in common.

Both of them were led to the swinging lifestyle by their spouses, although unlike Raquel, Noah was a willing participant. Also, both had been married several years without having kids. And although they'd met on an island resort thousands of miles away from home, they both were from Texas. Noah and his wife lived in Austin, and Raquel and Alexander lived only three hours away in Dallas.

The more they talked, the more Noah realized how vulnerable Raquel actually was. Her husband was taking advantage of her soft heart and her desire for a family. Noah wasn't some super hero swooping in to save a damsel in distress, but he did have an urgent need to knock some sense into Alexander. The man was as arrogant as they came. He strutted around the resort like he was God's gift to women. But somehow Giselle liked him, and it was merely a coincidence they had ended up with each other's spouse.

When Noah heard Raquel's steady breathing, he knew their all night pillow talk had come to an end. He reluctantly moved her off of his chest and took the glass from her hand and placed it on the bedside table.

Once Noah settled beside Raquel once again, she immediately snuggled close to his body. He wrapped his arms around her and fell into a sound restful sleep.

5

REDISCOVERY

Raquel woke up with a renewed disposition. The guilt she was feeling was gone and the shame was nowhere to be found. This swinging thing was what she'd agreed to, and Alexander was taking full advantage of the arrangement. So why shouldn't she?

Raquel knew that it was out of her character and not how she was raised, the whole subject was taboo, but when it came down to it, she didn't want to feel guilty for doing something she'd enjoyed. She realized society dictated a lot of how people responded to things, but she didn't want to care about society.

Why should she feel bad for sleeping with Noah? Alexander sure as hell didn't feel bad for sleeping with Giselle. He flaunted the blond around like his most prized possession. Raquel could still feel the remnants of anger just thinking about it. The level of carelessness her husband displayed was beyond disrespectful.

Raquel wanted to get out of her own head, so she decided to enjoy her surroundings. She was on a beautiful tropical island and it would be silly not to take it all in. She nodded to the staff as she walked along the colorful bungalows of the resort. The afternoon breeze was nice and it felt good against her heated skin. As she did the walk of shame, her heels clicking along the stones of the path, Raquel began to wonder if Alexander would even be in their room.

She closed the door softly as she took a deep breath. Raquel didn't know why she felt so hesitant. Her freedom from guilt was becoming fleeting and she began to feel the humiliation creep in.

"Alexander? Are you here?" Raquel called out as she made her way down the short hallway.

When there wasn't an answer, she didn't know if she should feel relieved or upset. She rounded the corner and saw the king sized bed was still eloquently made and the room was completely empty.

Raquel felt like a hypocrite for feeling pissed. After all, she was just getting back herself. She shook her head at her conflicting emotions. Usually Raquel was firm in her beliefs and decisions, she was not a wishy-washy woman. This back and forth was killing her, and she would be glad when they were able to go back home.

Raquel stripped out of her dress and heels, and got into the shower. The hot water relaxed her body as well as her thoughts. She was making herself sick with all the indecisiveness she was displaying since she'd been at the resort.

She needed to put her big girl panties on and face the facts. She could've told Alexander no. She could've told him that if he didn't give her a family, she wanted a divorce. She could've told him that he was ridiculous for asking her to become a swinger, and made him go to counseling. There had been so many options, but she'd chosen the easy way out.

It was time that she was realistic about what could truly happen to her marriage. And as much as she didn't want to admit Noah was right, he was. The empty room was proof; Alexander was living his best life while she was feeling guilty.

"No more of this nonsense. Time for a dose of reality. Have fun while you're here and deal with your sham of a marriage when you get home. You can do this, girl!" Raquel swiped the gel through her hair as she gave herself a much needed check.

They had five more days left on this beautiful island paradise, and she sure as hell wasn't going to spend it moping around feeling ashamed. Nope. *Hell no*! If Alexander could live his best life, so could she.

Raquel slipped on her bright yellow thong one piece before applying sunscreen. Her cover up was a sheer white sexy little number her husband had bought for her. She fluffed her short curls, grabbed her sunglasses and beach bag, and headed out the door.

Her steps felt lighter as she walked toward the beach. The sun was shining bright, and there were couples everywhere. Everyone was in different stages of undress. Some women were topless while others were completely nude. Most of the men were naked, and letting it all hang out for everyone to see.

Raquel laughed to herself. No matter how old the men were, they didn't seem to care about their bodies. And no matter how young the women were, their bodies were all they seemed to care about.

Everyone appeared to be peacocking for an audience, and although Raquel wanted no parts in the foolishness, she was still thoroughly entertained. She found a nice sun bed and umbrella with a nice view of the water. She sat down, pulled her book from her bag and made herself comfortable.

"Well, hey there, sunshine." The deep voice was sensual but one she didn't recognize.

Raquel looked up from her book, raising her sunglasses to sit on top of her head as she smiled at the silver fox standing in front of her. She wasn't sure how old the man was, but his body was impressive. He stood tall with nice lean legs and muscular arms. And although he didn't have a six pack, his flat stomach, and barreled chest showed he clearly worked out.

"Uh, hey..." Raquel waved awkwardly. This was the first time she had been alone on the beach, so she felt a little unsure.

The man sat down on the sun bed beside her, and she couldn't help but notice his manhood was standing up proudly. Raquel wondered if he had taken a little blue pill before his walk on the beach.

"So, I saw you last night. I didn't get a chance to tell you how sexy you looked." The man was bold, and Raquel was curious what else he had to say even if she wasn't interested in having sex with anyone else.

"Thank you." She replied simply.

"I saw you with Noah, and I was wondering if you would be up for a *new* companion tonight?" The man's smile reached his bright eyes, and Raquel could tell he was a charmer.

"No, I won't need a new companion tonight, but uh, thanks for asking." She smiled to soften the blow, but she wasn't sure how the charmer would react.

He continued to smile like she'd told him yes. "Well, if you change your mind, my name is Dane."

Dane held out his hand, and when Raquel took it, he kissed the back of hers with a sly smile.

She blushed prettily. "I'm Raquel. It's nice to meet you, Dane."

"Oh, the pleasure is *all* mine." Dane got up from his seat and his hard cock was eye level with Raquel. She shifted back in her seat as she looked up at Dane. He winked at her and turned and walked away.

"Old pervert." She chuckled.

One thing Raquel noticed was there was no lack of confidence from the men at the resort. And although she'd literally just had a stranger's dick in her face, most of the men were friendly and gave plenty of space to the women.

Raquel was probably the most uptight person at the resort, but she was determined to change that before she left. So instead of cussing Dane out, and calling him every name under the sun, she chuckled. She had to pat herself on the back for newfound openness.

⚘

RAQUEL SPENT MOST OF THE DAY LOUNGING ON THE BEACH, SIPPING piña coladas, snacking and most importantly, people watching. If she wasn't trying not to be so judgmental, she would call this place the devil's playground.

The people were frolicking around in the water and on the sandy beach, playing volleyball, soaking up the sun, and sipping fruity drinks adorned with tiny umbrellas. And all of this was done completely nude. Now, being nude wasn't what made these things sinful. No. Raquel thought it was amusing to watch, but there were some people who weren't just frolicking. Some people were getting blowjobs by the poolside while others were just flat out having sex.

Raquel tried not to watch, but it was like resisting watching a World Star video. Yeah, you knew you shouldn't be watching it or condoning ratchet behavior, but you just couldn't seem to help yourself.

Raquel didn't consider herself a voyeur, but she couldn't tear her eyes away from the couple having sex on the sun bed twenty feet from her in broad daylight. She was happy to have on her large sunglasses because she was sure her wide-eyed stare would interrupt their groove.

When the woman looked up and licked her lips in Raquel's direction, she decided it was probably time for her to leave the beach for the day.

Raquel gathered up her bag and slipped on her flip flops before making her way up to the pool. The pool area was way more lively with music and games and bartenders doing tricks. She found a vacant sun bed and sat down.

"Hola, señorita. Would you like a drink and a towel?" Raquel smiled at how quick the service was. It was one thing she truly enjoyed about the resort.

"Hola, señor. Si, I would love a frozen strawberry margarita to drink, gracias." Raquel responded still wearing a bright smile.

"De nada." The waiter nodded politely as he hurried away.

Raquel relaxed against the chair as she chuckled at the shenanigans of the game participants. Watching grown people try to move a ball from their torso up to their mouths without using their hands was pretty damn entertaining.

"Well, you look like you're enjoying yourself." The deep voice sounded from behind her. Raquel didn't want to see his face, so she didn't bother to turn around.

"Did you think I wouldn't?" She questioned without turning around her tone dry.

"What's the sour mood about?" Alexander started to massage her shoulders.

Raquel shook him off. She wasn't in the mood for his bullshit. It was near one in the afternoon and he was just now showing his face. The audacity of him to pretend like everything was peaches and cream.

"Oh so you know me now?" Raquel snapped as she turned around to face him.

"Aww come on, babe." He held up his hands with a smirk on his handsome face, his eyes crinkling at the corners. "I was with Giselle. Why are you acting like we didn't agree to this?"

"Don't come on babe me. I know what we agreed to, but I didn't know you were going to completely ignore me last night. What the hell was that about?"

"I didn't ignore you." Alexander furrowed his brows in fake confusion.

Raquel gave him the side eye so hard that she almost got a headache. "Well, what would you call not speaking to your wife all night? I wouldn't say it was you being an attentive husband."

"Hey, listen, babe. I didn't know you were going to be so sensitive about this. I thought you were having fun with Noah." Alexander shrugged nonchalantly.

She couldn't believe that her husband was so dense. "Having fun" with Noah had nothing to do with not speaking to her. What the fuck was he smoking in Jamaica? He had to be high.

"First of all, I'm not being fucking sensitive. It is not unusual for me to want my fucking husband to speak to me when he sees me. Just because I agreed to do this shit doesn't mean you can run off and lose your fucking mind." Raquel was really and truly pissed off. This wasn't even about their agreement. It was all about respecting her as his wife.

"Whoa, Raquel! Since when do you curse at me? This isn't how we talk to each other." Alexander scowled at her, but Raquel didn't care. If he could treat her any kind of way, then she could talk to him in the same manner.

Raquel took a deep, calming breath. "A whole lot of how we *used* to treat each other has changed. So let's not pretend to be the perfect little couple."

"Well, I guess this is the wrong time to bring up swapping for the rest of our stay?" Alexander sighed heavily. The noise only served to further enrage Raquel.

"You know what? Let's do it. I agreed to this, and Noah knows how to put it down. No sense in wasting a free pass." Raquel knew she was being petty, but to hell with Alexander and his wife swapping heathen ass.

"See you later or maybe not. Whatever." Raquel threw over her shoulder as she grabbed her beach bag.

"Raquel! Raquel!" She heard Alexander calling her name, but she continued to saunter away without looking back.

Raquel was mad, but when she saw the waiter coming with her drink she smiled. She never broke stride as she scooped up her drink and nodded to the waiter. The least should could do was enjoy a refreshing beverage before she jumped head first into sin.

⚜ 6 ⚜

CONNECTIONS

Noah spent most of the day lounging around and reminiscing. He couldn't get last night and this morning out of his head. He kept replaying Raquel's moans of ecstasy, the breathless sound of his name from her lips, and even her satisfied grin.

Thoughts of Raquel danced through his head even when Giselle came sashaying into their bungalow with a big smile plastered on her face.

Noah didn't even ask her how her night was. They usually rehashed everything, per Giselle's insistence. She got off on retelling her exploits to Noah. It didn't bother him, though. He just wanted to make his wife happy. It wasn't like he wasn't enjoying himself as well, but he didn't have to tell her everything that he did while she wasn't there. As a matter of fact, she never asked him what he did.

"How was your evening, honey?" Giselle asked sweetly. He knew that she didn't really want to know. She just asked so he would ask her in return.

Noah almost wanted to roll his eyes, but grown ass men didn't do that. "My night was good. What about yours?"

"Oh, honey, let me tell you. "As Giselle went into vivid detail about her wild night, Noah tuned her out, still thinking about when or if he would get the chance to see Raquel again.

Noah nodded and agreed at the appropriate times. He still wasn't truly listening until Giselle's words broke into his thoughts.

"I just feel a connection with Alexander, so I think we should swap for the rest of the trip because there's no sense exploring anyone else." Giselle smiled brightly.

"Did you say swap for the rest of the trip?" Noah tried to dampen his excitement.

"Yeah. I mean we've done it before. I just thought since it worked so well the last time, we could do it again." Giselle was giving him her best puppy dog eyes and pouty lips.

Little did she know, she didn't have to try so hard to convince him. Hell, he was ready to leave her ass standing in his dust. He was so excited to have Raquel for the rest of the stay at the resort that he had to think baseball stats so his dick wouldn't get hard.

"If that's what you want to do, sweetheart. You know I'll do anything to make you happy." Noah finally responded, using his most calming voice and sweetest smile.

He couldn't have imagined he would get the chance to spend more time with Raquel. Maybe he would get over the slight obsession he was beginning to form. He could use this extra time to get her completely out of his system.

Giselle squealed in delight, clapping her hands and jumping up and down like she was a damn seal. His wife could be a bit childish at times, but Noah chose to overlook it. They'd been together for so long he was simply used to her shenanigans.

"Let's get dressed for the beach and I'll let Alex know what we decided." She squealed again as she ran off to get changed.

Noah didn't have to change because he'd been lounging all day. He'd just so happened to come back to their bungalow for sunscreen. He had no idea where Giselle had been, and he didn't actually care. On these vacations, they pretty much did their own thing.

Once they got down to the beach, Noah found a couple of sun beds and got comfortable. Giselle sat her bag down, and quickly went in search of "Alex." Noah guessed he wasn't the only one giving out nicknames because he was sure Raquel only called her husband by his full name. He shrugged because it should've bothered him more that his wife was so eager to spend time with another man, but in all actuality, it didn't.

And even though they were swingers, any other time her behavior would have irked him. However, he was so preoccupied with getting another taste of Raquel he couldn't pay his wife much attention.

Noah casually looked around when he saw glistening cocoa skin marching in the direction of the pool bar. He slid his sunglasses over his eyes and quickly strode in her direction. Her long legs and fast pace had him running to catch up with her.

"Rocky! Hey!" Noah shouted to get her attention. She stopped abruptly and turned around with a big smile plastered across her face.

He couldn't decipher if the smile was real or not because the oversized shades covered her onyx eyes.

"Hey, Noah. What's up?" Her stance was more relaxed than he'd seen her but something still seemed off about her demeanor.

"I just want to talk to you. I talked with Giselle..." Noah stopped talking when she held up her finely manicured hand.

"I talked to Alexander. He told me what they want." Noah still couldn't read her mood to know if she was angry, but she didn't seem too thrilled.

"Okay. But what do *you* want?" Noah questioned slowly, not wanting to piss her off.

"I told him it was a great fucking idea. Why not sleep with someone else's husband for the rest of our swingers' get away. Why the hell not? That's what we're here for, right?" She pursed her lips and then smiled.

"So, I'm guessing that's a *no*?" He relaxed at the smile on her face.

"No. I mean it's a *yes*. He wants to live it up, so I should too." She shrugged.

Noah could tell Raquel was trying to pull off nonchalance, but he could see right through her. She wasn't all the way on board with the idea.

"Okay, but you know that you don't have to do this. It's still *your* choice." When she took off her sunglasses and pinched the bridge of her nose hanging her head, he softly placed his hand under her chin and raised it. He wanted to see those midnight eyes. Noah needed to make sure she knew he was telling her the truth.

"I'm serious. Just because Giselle and Alexander want to swap, doesn't mean you have to feel pressure to stay with me. If you say no, then it's no. Understand?" Noah questioned, still looking deep in her eyes.

Raquel sighed heavily before nodding. Noah still wasn't convinced that she was completely comfortable with the idea. But he wouldn't hound her because that wasn't his style. He'd rather watch her closely and act accordingly.

NOAH PACKED UP HIS BAG TO MOVE IN WITH RAQUEL. DOING A FULL swap wasn't complex. The women would stay in their bungalows, and their male companions would go to them. They would swap back on the morning of departure.

Giselle had left the room to meet Alexander at one of the hotel bars, so Noah was alone in the room. He was glad he had some peace and quiet, so he could get his mind ready for the next few days.

No other woman ever had his mind so twisted before. He wanted to do all the nasty dirty things he'd been thinking since she left him that morning. Even though they'd had all types of sex, it still wasn't enough to satisfy his appetite for the vivacious temptress.

Noah made his way down the winding path and up to the bright yellow bungalow. He knocked on the door and waited impatiently. He had to hold back from banging on the door like he was the police.

After a brief minute, Raquel opened the door wearing a beautiful smile that lit up her face. She was truly a remarkable beauty.

"Hi." She opened the door wider so he could enter.

"Hey, beautiful." Noah leaned down and kissed her soft cheek.

He entered the bungalow and looked around. All the rooms had the same tropical décor, but the bed looked slightly smaller and it was facing the open balcony. Noah wasn't a small guy, so he frowned at the queen sized bed. However, when Raquel sauntered past him and sat down on it, all thoughts of bed sizes vanished from his mind.

"So, how do you want to do this?" Raquel asked with a look of curiosity in her eyes.

Noah sat down beside her. He couldn't help the smile that graced his lips as he gently caressed her cheek with the back of his hand. "We just go with the flow. No pressure to do anything. We're here to have fun. Let's get to know each other a little better over the next few days, and we can do whatever the hell we wanna do, darlin'. How's that sound?" Noah questioned seriously.

Raquel nodded with a large smile. "That sounds great. No pressure?"

"Right." Noah nodded in return.

They decided to start their little adventure with a visit to the pool bar. It was late afternoon and the pool activities were winding down. There was still loud chatter and laughter, and everyone seemed to be having a great time; including Alexander and Giselle.

Noah knew the exact moment when Raquel spotted her husband tonguing down Giselle because she paused mid-step and her entire body tensed. Noah instinctively grabbed her hand as he leaned down and kissed her on the side of her neck.

He felt her body relax before she continued walking. She held his hand tightly as they maneuvered through the crowd and found sun beds. They placed their beach bags down and Noah adjusted the umbrella. They ordered drinks and a late lunch and sat to watch the entertainment.

Diamonds was a nudist resort, but nudity wasn't mandatory. The majority of the people were naked, but some women were just topless. Noah watched as Raquel took a deep breath and took off her bathing suit. It was the first time he'd seen her go completely nude at the pool.

She was loosening up, and Noah was appreciative, especially of the view. Raquel's curves were extraordinary. She was reminiscent of the old pinup models. She was all hips, breasts, and legs that went on forever. Noah was in hog heaven.

Noah was relaxing with his drink in hand when he heard a man's voice trying but failing miserably to chat up Raquel. The man had a head full of gray hair and he was pretty well built. He was talking to Raquel as if they were familiar. So Noah gave the conversation his full attention.

"Did you all just get here? I don't think I've seen you before," the man said.

Raquel's eyes were again covered by large sunglasses, so Noah couldn't completely read the expression on her face.

"No. We've been here a week already." Raquel shrugged.

"Oh! I'm not sure how I missed an exotic beauty like you. I must've had too many margaritas the last couple of days." He chuckled.

Noah shook his head. Calling one of the few black women at the resort "exotic" was definitely unoriginal.

"Well, like I said I've been here so I'm really not sure how you missed me." Raquel giggled.

Noah raised an eyebrow. He wasn't certain, but he was pretty sure Raquel was flirting with this lame dude.

"Honey, like I said, I had to have been completely out of my mind to have missed that gorgeous face, and beautiful body. Hmmm uh." The man hummed and licked his lips.

Noah guessed he was trying to be seductive, but he really just looked like a degenerate. Noah frowned at his thoughts. He never felt jealous before, but this feeling was definitely envy. Weird.

Noah heard Raquel giggle again, and his frown deepened.

"I'm sorry, lovely lady. I was so distracted by your beauty I didn't ask you your name." Noah noticed the man's smile was predatory, and he knew it was time for him to step in.

"Her name is Raquel, and I'm Noah." He smirked at the man.

The guy turned his head and nodded. "It's nice to meet you all. I'm Ernie."

"Nice to meet you as well, Ernie." Raquel sweetly responded.

She seemed more comfortable than ever, especially since Ernie's junk was waving in her face their entire conversation. Yet, she only giggled and smiled. The woman he'd first met would've balked at the audacity of the man, but this version of Raquel was actually relaxed.

Noah once again smiled. If Raquel continued to be this relaxed, these next few days were going to be better than he'd expected.

7

THE SWING OF THINGS

Once Raquel decided she wasn't going to worry about what Alexander was doing, she finally relaxed. There was one thing about Raquel. As soon as she made up her mind there was no changing it. She could feel herself loosening up, and the first thing she saw after her miraculous decision was her husband kissing Giselle so hard it looked as if he were trying to swallow her entire face. The scene instantly made her tense up all over again. It also made her think.

Alexander had taken to the swinging life style so quickly and with such enthusiasm that he'd dismissed her feelings. Raquel knew her husband had a tendency to be selfish, but this trip was bringing out the worst in him. Or maybe she was finally able to see through his bullshit and see him for the asshole he actually was. Either way, Raquel knew after this trip their relationship would never be the same. *She* would never be the same.

No matter if she changed for better or worse, she pushed her reservations to the back of her mind because she was determined to make the best out of the rest of her vacation. In two weeks, she would have to return back to work, and being a school counselor could be extremely stressful. She needed every bit of her vacation time to decompress, and so far she had wasted it by being uptight.

So, when Mr. Easy Ernie came along trying to flirt, Raquel decided to play along. There was no need in being so rigid, especially in a place like this. Yes, most of the men at the resort were horny bastards, but they were harmless. And she had to admit it was kind of flattering being hit on even if all they wanted was sex. Besides, people came to the resort for fun and apparently, lots of sex, so she was sure that the people didn't shy away from a little flirting and neither should she.

And even though she was one of the few black women at the resort, she didn't feel mistreated or uncomfortable. Well, at least not uncomfortable because of how anyone spoke to her. The nakedness was definitely something she had to overcome, but the more she saw people in the nude, the more used to it she became.

Before Raquel could finish her conversation with Ernie, another man smoothly approached. It seemed as if Ernie's bravery broke the ice and everyone else decided to shoot their shot. She could hear Noah grumble next to her, but she simply smirked. If she was to get into this swinging thing for the rest of her stay, she might as well talk to other people. It wasn't like she had to sleep with any of them, but the least she could do was be more social.

Raquel knew that she was uptight and from the time they stepped foot onto the resort she was acting like her entire world was ending. Even though her marriage might come to an end, it didn't mean her world should. After they left, Raquel would figure out what needed to be done about her marriage, but for now, she would participate in the iniquity that was going on around her. The people were friendly and everyone looked like they were having the time of their lives, so she could do the same.

"You are truly a beautiful woman." The new guy complimented, breaking into Raquel's wandering thoughts.

"Well, thank you." She smiled brightly at the dark haired man with sparkling eyes.

His face was gorgeous with dark features and a mischievous smile. His body was lean and cut in all the right places. Raquel snuck a peek at his manhood, and although he wasn't huge, he was still impressive.

"My name is Garret."

"Nice to meet you. I'm Raquel."

"Are you guys going to the Gods and Goddesses theme party tonight?" Garret asked, looking toward Noah.

Raquel turned to gage Noah's reaction since he'd been quietly brooding since Ernie had introduced himself. "Of course, we're going. The best part of this place are the theme parties." Raquel excitedly responded.

When she looked at Noah for confirmation, he nodded with a smile that stole her breath. It was all straight white teeth and dimples, and those arresting eyes that held her captive were going to be a problem.

Raquel managed to break her gaze away from Noah to continue her conversation with Garret. His wife, Dayna, eventually joined them, and Raquel had to admit that they were some of the nicest people she'd ever met on vacation.

Later, when the party at the pool had somewhat died down, she lay relaxing under the large umbrella. Raquel smirked to herself at the thought of all the naked people she'd had casual conversations with. She was proud of herself for being social and nonjudgmental.

"What put that little smirk on your face?" Noah's deep voice was sensual in her ear.

Raquel had no idea when he moved so close to her, but she didn't hate the giddy feeling that had overtaken her.

"Just thinking how I wanted to let loose and I actually did it." She turned her head and their faces were so close she couldn't help but brush her lips against his softly.

The light touch turned into a heated kiss when Noah slid his hand to grip the back of her neck; pulling her closer and devouring her lips.

Raquel's body instantly reacted, and her body temperature rose with each twirl of his masterful tongue. She gripped his long hair tightly as she reveled in the feel of his bare chest flushed against her naked breasts.

The smattering of soft hair on his muscular chest had her nipples hardening with desire. Noah's groan into her mouth snapped her out of her lustful thoughts. A few more seconds and Raquel would've been riding Noah's cock poolside. She had relaxed a little, but she wasn't that far gone.

"I think we should go back to the room." Raquel's voice came out throaty and aroused. She didn't even recognize the sound.

"I think that's the best damn thing you've said all day, darlin'." Noah responded grabbing up their things and rushing back to the bungalow.

Raquel knew that the sex they were about to have was going to be different than before. It wasn't about the new experience or the comfort. It was about lust. Pure and simple. And she couldn't wait.

⚜

ONCE THEY MADE IT BACK TO THE BUNGALOW, THE COUPLE DIDN'T waste any time with formalities. They were all over each other from the time they crossed the threshold. There weren't any clothes in the way, so they fell onto the bed in a sensual heap of caresses, kisses, and limbs.

A smiling Noah tossed a giggling Raquel on the bed, and she flopped down with a soft thud. Although there was plenty of sexual tension between them, the mood was still playful and fun.

Noah growled as he crawled up her body, licking and sucking every inch of her skin until he reached her mouth. His tongue tasted every inch until she was gasping from the immense pleasure.

However, Noah didn't let up. He kissed the hollow of her neck and then nibbled on her collar bone. Every time he touched her, Raquel felt like she was being zapped with electricity. Her body was on fire and her thighs were slick with her arousal.

Noah trailed his curious fingers down her body into the heated valley between her legs. "Shit, darlin', you're soakin' wet."

"Don't tease me." Raquel warned. She was so turned on and ready that the word wait was not in her vocabulary. She would gladly get on top and ride him until the sun set if that's what it would take. But she refused to let him torment her like he did when she was tied to the bed. This was a different rodeo, and she was ready to ride a cowboy.

"What's the matter, darlin'? You can't handle the..."

Noah didn't finish his sentence because Raquel caught him by surprise and bucked him off of her. She hastily climbed on top and her smile grew at the wide-eyed expression on his handsome face.

"I said," she kissed his lips. "Don't. Tease. Me." With each word she pecked his lips.

"Oh, so you want to be in control, huh?" Noah chuckled, placing his muscular arms behind his head. Raquel felt the sudden urge to lick him from head to toe. So, she did.

Noah groaned deep in his throat, and the sound made Raquel wetter. She reached to the bedside table and pulled out the protection, and slid it on his hard throbbing cock without hesitation.

The night before they had gotten carried away, and they had forgotten to use protection. They both were clean health wise, and although Raquel was no longer on the pill, it hadn't been that long since she'd stopped taking them, so she wasn't worried. However, she had to make sure there weren't any more slip ups.

Raquel slid her tight wet pussy down on Noah's pulsating cock. She felt every ridge and vein in his massive member. The feeling of him inside her was exquisite. As she moved her curvaceous body up and down she could feel her insides quiver.

Noah soon took over, as he began to pump into her hot canal from beneath. His large hands held her waist in a death grip. Raquel knew she would have bruises because he was holding her so tight, but she didn't care.

She was in the throes of ecstasy and she was a slave to the desire. Noah was making her body sing with every stroke of his magnificent member. Raquel clawed his back and screamed his name, and he continued to give her everything she needed.

"Give me this pussy. Yes, baby! Scream my name! Fuck! Rocky, you feel so fucking good."

Noah's words were clear, and Raquel wanted to respond. But the dick was so good her brain and mouth weren't cooperating. So all she could do was grunt and hang on as he rode her body to the brink of bliss.

"I'm... shit! I... cum..." Raquel couldn't even complete a sentence but Noah got the message because he slipped his hand between their sweat soaked bodies and began to toy with her clit.

He applied just the right amount of pressure to send her body reeling. Her long, shapely legs began to shake as they tightened around his waist. Raquel's head was thrown back in elation and sweat peppered her brow. The feeling of pure bliss built until she couldn't hold off the orgasm any longer.

Raquel's arms were wrapped tightly around Noah's neck as she took his long cock. She released a loud scream as she exploded. Her pussy gushed and clenched tightly around Noah's dick. His continued thrusting, prolonged her orgasm and her body didn't come down for what seemed like hours.

Noah's pace picked up as he thrust wildly into Raquel's sopping wet pussy. He laid her on her back and continued to stroke her into oblivion. Raquel could only thrash her head from side to side and moan out her pleasure.

Noah was a beast in the bed, and Raquel had to thank her lucky stars that she ended up with him. It would've been a travesty to come to a sexy resort and end up with someone as bland as her husband was.

"Fuck, Rocky! Your pussy is so good!" Noah roared as sweat dripped from his body.

"Yes, Noah! Shit!" Raquel screamed as he pushed into her so hard that it sent shivers down her spine.

His orgasm was so powerful that Raquel felt the rippling of his cum through the condom. It was the best sex she had ever had, and the day wasn't even done yet.

❧ 8 ❧

IT'S ALL SEXUAL

Noah couldn't believe just how sexy Raquel was in her goddess getup. The white, lacey, see through lingerie with a sheer wrap around skirt and gold accessories made her look like a walking, talking Athena.

The headband she wore on her short curls looked like a golden crown. Her long legs were accentuated by gold gladiator heels that wrapped around her calves. The bangles she wore jangled as she moved gracefully toward him.

"How do I look?" She slowly twirled around in a circle, giving Noah a three-sixty view of her magnificence.

"You look..." Noah ran a hand through his long hair to get himself together. His heart beat rapidly and his cock pulsated in his pants. He was ready to tear through Raquel's outfit and ravage her on the floor like a caveman.

"You look fuckin' edible, darlin'."

Noah could see the heat of blush in her cheeks, and he smiled at her reaction. She was so fuckin' beautiful and innocent. It was almost a shame for him to corrupt her. *Almost.*

"Thank you, Noah. You look pretty freaking hot yourself." Her eyes twinkled with her beautiful smile.

Noah smirked at her assessment. He knew that he looked good. Hell, he spent hours in the gym so his body would be immaculate. At almost forty, it wasn't as easy as it used to be to stay in shape, but with hard work and a healthy diet, his six pack was still intact and his muscular physique was on point.

His gold god outfit was all Giselle, though, and there wasn't much to it. Instead of a traditional gladiator skirt, he wore tight white shorts with a gold belt, gold cuffs, gold cape, and a sword. His bare chest was out for all to see, and he didn't necessarily hate the attention; especially from Raquel.

"Thank you, darlin'. Let's head to the bar so we can get a couple of drinks before the show starts."

The couple headed down to the lobby of the resort where the open bar and theater were located. Noah could see that Raquel felt confident in her goddess outfit as she held her head high and strutted in front of him like a queen.

He watched the sway of her round hips and ass, and he was glad that the resort was for erotic fun because walking around with a massive hard-on would not be acceptable anywhere else.

When they made it to the lobby bar, it was packed with everyone in their best goddess and god costumes. Raquel's demeanor changed from sexy vixen to giddy kid in seconds. Her face lit up and her head looked from left to right and back again.

"So I take it you're a costume party person?" Noah's smile mirrored Raquel's. He could feel the happiness rolling off her and he was glad he could witness the change in her.

"I love a good theme party! And everybody here participates. It's so awesome!" She replied excitedly, still looking around.

Noah maneuvered them through the large crowd to the bar. He ordered drinks as he leaned against the sleek mirrored top to wait on the bartender. Raquel was in yet another conversation with a gawking male, and Noah felt another hit of jealousy.

"So, I see you're enjoying *my* wife." He heard the smug voice before he turned to see the little man standing behind him.

"Oh yeah. Your wife is absolutely delectable. I have to thank you for convincing her to come." Noah licked his lips as he smiled wickedly as Alexander's face turned red.

Noah thought to himself. *How could a man who talked his wife into something, and ignores her almost the entirety of the trip, act jealous? The arrogant asshole had a lot of nerve.*

"Well, I'm definitely enjoying your wife. She's a wild one."

Noah knew Alexander was trying to get under his skin, but that shit definitely wouldn't work on him. Giselle was *not* like Raquel. She'd always been a "free spirit," and Noah tended to give her whatever she wanted. They weren't brand new to swinging, and the only woman Noah seemed to get jealous over was Raquel. *Ironic.*

"Yes." Noah chuckled. "Giselle has always been *adventurous.* She likes to give her all to an experience. I'm glad to hear she's enjoying herself. Otherwise, I wouldn't be able to *enjoy* myself." Noah winked and he could tell by the frown on the other man's face that his words had struck a chord.

Alexander simply grunted as he walked away. He headed toward Raquel, and Noah almost followed him until he felt a hand slide down his back. He turned to see a petite brunette smiling up at him.

He had seen the woman before and he'd even talked to her, but for the life of him, he couldn't remember her name.

"Hello there, handsome." She smiled seductively as Noah gave her the attention she was obviously after.

"Hey, sugar. Don't you look sweet?" Noah smiled, playing up his infamous charm. He would rather be watching the interaction between Raquel and Alexander, but he knew he would act like a jealous asshole, and he couldn't let himself go there. Instead, Noah decided to entertain a woman he had absolutely no interest in, so he could keep his cool.

The woman blushed prettily, her tan cheeks turning pink. And even though Noah wasn't interested in her beyond this particular exchange, he had to admit she was quite stunning.

"My name is Rose. You're Noah, right?"

"Right. It's nice to meet you, Rose. You're the hostess that checked us in." Noah stated, finally recalling where he'd seen her.

Rose was dressed similar to the other ladies in her goddess outfit, which surprised Noah. Usually the daytime employees didn't work at night, and they definitely didn't participate in the offered "activities." However, Noah brushed it off and continued to smile down at the petite woman.

"You know I've seen you around and I have to say you're quite sexy." Rose brushed up against him, and Noah raised his brows in shock.

There was an unwritten rule about not flirting too heavily with the staff, but people usually disregarded it. There was nothing wrong with a little flirting, but everyone knew not to cross the line because there was definitely a no fraternizing policy.

Rose's small hand caressed his chest as a smile covered her face. Noah could tell that she definitely wasn't new to the act of seduction.

"Okay, ladies and gentlemen, the doors are now open!" The host of the nightly theme party threw open the doors to the theater dramatically. The interruption was welcomed as Noah smiled down at a frowning Rose.

"Well, that's my cue to find my date. You have a good night, sugar." Noah nodded and walked away.

He found Raquel waiting by the door and he took her hand and led her inside the room.

ONCE THEY FOUND THEIR SEATS, THE LIGHTS WERE SLOWLY DIMMED. A spotlight appeared on the circular dance floor that was surrounded by the crowd. The light swooped from the floor to the vaulted ceiling where a woman dressed in all white was floating like an angel. She was suspended from silk ropes high over the crowd. Her dark hair was pulled back from her face in a long braid with gold ribbon weaved throughout.

As she floated elegantly from the ceiling, using the silk, the pulsating beat of the music made her decent look erotic. Her body flipped and turned in sensual displays of grace. Noah watched Raquel's face light up and her eyes brighten as she watched the acrobat.

When the woman made her way back to the ceiling and did a dramatic drop, catching herself right before she hit the floor, Raquel gasped loudly and clutched Noah's hand tightly. Her eyes were round in awe and Noah smiled and kissed the corner of her mouth.

"Oh my goodness! She was amazing!" Raquel leaned in, speaking directly into his ear.

"Just wait until the next act." Noah smiled as he nodded toward the dance floor. Raquel happily turned around to watch the rest of the show, still holding Noah's hand.

After all the entertainment had finished, the DJ turned up the music and the couples began to flood the floor. Noah let Raquel pull him onto the floor and they began to dance to the music. Raquel was smiling and laughing as she held her hands over her head and danced freely. Noah pulled her against his body as they continued to move. Her joyous mood was contagious and he couldn't help but want to be as close to her as possible.

"I hate to interrupt, but I thought my wife might want to dance with me at least once."

Noah shook his head at Alexander's antics. There was no way a guy like him was cut out for the swinging life style. As long as his wife was miserable and pining after him, he was fine. But as soon as she started to relax and show interest in Noah, it was a problem.

"I've already told you, Alexander. This is what *you* wanted. Now go to your little plaything and have a good time." Raquel turned back around and continued to dance, but Alexander wasn't going to go away so easily.

Alexander grabbed Raquel's wrist so she would face him again as he yelled in her face, "What the hell is wrong with you? Why are you trying to embarrass me?"

"Hey, asshole, let her go!" Noah stepped up and pushed the snarling man back. The move effectively loosened his grip on Raquel as he stumbled backward.

"Who the fuck do you think you are?" Alexander righted himself, but he didn't move to retaliate against a much larger Noah.

Before Noah could respond, Giselle made an appearance. Her eyes narrowed on Noah. "What's going on here? Alexander?" She questioned, looking from Noah to Alexander.

"Your husband needs to mind his fucking business! That's what's going on!" Alexander shouted, looking like his head was about to explode.

Noah could only guess that the man wasn't challenged very often. And he knew for a fact that Raquel did any and every thing she possibly could to keep him happy, so for her to dismiss him must've been a rude awakening.

"Noah? You know we don't get involved in other people's marital bullshit." Giselle chastised as if she were his mother.

"Giselle," Noah said, slowly trying to rein in his temper. "You don't know what the fuck is going on, so I suggest you take your *little* buddy for a walk before I rock his ass to sleep."

Giselle frowned, but she grabbed Alexander and pulled him away. He went willingly with a scowl on his face, but he didn't say anything else. Noah knew that the coward didn't want any problems, and Giselle knew that Noah didn't make idle threats.

"Hey, you okay?" Noah questioned as he wrapped his arms around Raquel.

"I'm fine." She sighed. "I just don't know what he wants from me. First, he's pushing me into your arms, then he wants me to get away from you." Raquel shook her head. "I'm tired of trying to figure him out. Let's enjoy the rest of tonight and tomorrow. I'll deal with Alexander when we get back home."

"Sounds like a good idea, but remember I'm here if you want to talk. I don't know what's up with your husband, but the way he manhandled you was bullshit."

Raquel nodded. "I know. He's never grabbed me like that before. He doesn't abuse me if that's what you think."

Noah put his hands up in surrender. That's exactly what he thought, but he wouldn't express his concerns because it was obvious Raquel didn't trust him enough. However, he trusted her, and if she said Alexander didn't hit her, then he didn't. But it was more than one way to abuse someone, and it definitely seemed like Raquel was on the receiving end of emotional and verbal abuse.

"Let's go relax in the hot tub, and then I can make you forget all about this shit." Noah smiled charmingly and Raquel gave him a small smile in return.

"Alright. Let's go."

9

SAYING GOODBYE

Raquel didn't think that saying goodbye to Noah would be difficult, but after all of the time he'd spent ravishing her body, catering to her every sexual desire, and just simply being there for her, difficult wasn't even a strong enough word to express how hard the goodbye had been.

They didn't make any silly promises or exchange contact information. They weren't fooling themselves by pretending they'd had some grand love affair. Noah provided her with the safe place she'd needed while being in over her head. He was a nice guy who didn't mix words. He'd told her the truth bluntly without apologies and the best thing of all, he had given her multiple orgasms.

Raquel didn't want to regret her time with Noah, but she did feel ashamed that she enjoyed it so much. She told herself she was doing this to save her marriage, but going to the resort was against everything she believed. She never considered swinging in her life. She hadn't even known there were special places for that type of thing. But the shame had crept in because in actuality, she'd had fun once she loosened up and ignored Alexander's antics.

She sat quietly in her window seat looking out at the runway. She did her best to let the sounds of the airport distract her. The tension between her and Alexander was thick and it was overshadowing the last few blissful days with Noah. But with every huff and narrowed eyed glance from her husband, she knew the bliss was long gone.

It was beyond stupid of her to think that running off to a swinger's resort was going to fix their intimacy and communication issues. It was even more insane to think about bringing a child into the mess. She continued to gaze out the window, hoping that things would turn around.

"Close the window. The sun is shining in my eyes." Alexander seemed to have a permanent frown on his face, and he had been in a sour mood all morning.

Raquel really wanted things to be okay between them, but she was already tired of Alexander's bullshit, so she ignored him.

Although their vacation wasn't what she wanted, it was exactly what she needed. It opened her eyes to just how awful she let her husband treat her. She had been in denial for a long time and trying to make her marriage work that she overlooked the obvious. Alexander didn't want to be married... at least not to her. And that was something she had to wrap her head around.

They had been together for such a long time. Raquel had lost her identity. She was so busy being Alexander's wife, she neglected to be Raquel.

"Who was that woman you were talking to?" Raquel asked Alexander. They were at her holiday party for her school district, and Alexander had disappeared. When Raquel finally found him almost an hour later she'd seen him with a short brunette from across the room. His hand was on the woman's waist and he was whispering in her ear. The scene was far too intimate for two strangers.

"Nobody." Alexander tersely answered with a frown on his face.

"Well, you were awfully close for that to have been nobody." Raquel crossed her arms over her chest defensively. He'd practically left her alone at the party to talk to "nobody" it was hurtful.

"Don't start with your insecurities, Raquel. I told you it was nobody. I swear any time I talk to another woman you behave like a bitch." Alexander whispered the hateful words in her ear. From the outside looking in, it would

seem like a loving husband whispering sweet nothings to a doting wife. It was far from the truth.

Raquel refused to let the tears come to her eyes, they would only give her husband more reasons to be cruel. She didn't want to be a weak woman or inse-cure, and she had known when she married him that Alexander was a flirt. She chose to ignore his ways, and now she was paying for it.

"I'm not being a bitch, Alexander. I just wanted to know who my husband was talking to. I didn't know you knew anyone here." Raquel's voice was soft. She didn't want to argue with her husband especially while they were around her colleagues. But anyone could see that Alexander's behavior with the brunette was inappropriate for a married man.

"I know a lot of people, Raquel. Stop acting so juvenile. I was just having a friendly conversation. Jesus, it's like you watch my every move." Alexander stormed away, and Raquel was left feeling helpless. In the past few months, everything set him off, it was as if he were looking for reasons to be upset with her.

Raquel had done everything in her power to not rock the boat. She wanted her loving and attentive husband back, so she resolved herself to pleasing, Alexander. And maybe the man she loved would show up again.

"Are you going to shut the window or what?" Alexander growled once again bringing Raquel out of her depressing memories.

Raquel slowly turned to face her husband with a sweet smile. "Does it look like I made any move to shut the window? I'm looking out of it. If it bothers you so much, then turn and face the other fucking direction."

Alexander's brows furrowed as if he couldn't believe Raquel had spoken to him in such a manner. It had to have been a shock to him because she never challenged her husband in any way. In the past, she would immediately back down, so she wouldn't upset her husband. She was always trying to please him. *What a waste of time.* Raquel turned her gaze to the scenery outside her window, thinking hard about what she should do next.

The rest of the trip was spent in silence as they traveled through customs, and home to the suburbs of Dallas. Alexander was brooding and pouting like the big man baby that he was, and Raquel spent the time forgiving herself for making bad decisions and not seeing her husband for who he was in the past.

She couldn't blame Alexander for everything because she was a grown woman and she chose to go to Diamond's Resort. She tried to bargain her way into having the family she wanted, instead of looking at the real problems in her marriage.

Now she was ready to face the music. Her marriage was crumbling and she could either work with her husband to save it, or leave it.

"So we're just not talking now, is that it?" Alexander grumbled as he sat the luggage down in their bedroom.

"I've never known you to hold back anything you wanted to say before. So if you want to talk, talk." Raquel crossed her arms over her ample chest with an arched brow.

"You don't have to get smart, Raquel. What's gotten into you?"

"Another man's dick! That's what!" Raquel shouted, losing all of her cool. "What? You didn't think that shit would change our relationship? Are you dumb?"

"Raquel, don't try to put all this on me. You were ready and willing, and it took no time at all for you to hop in the bed with *Noah*." Alexander snarled the other man's name like a curse.

"Ready and willing? You're in-fucking-sane!" Raquel replied exasperated. "It's not all your fault, but I sure as hell wasn't *ready and willing.*"

"Don't try to play innocent with me. I know you, *Raquel.* You wanted this as much as I did. You just wanted to pretend to be all high and mighty about it. Blaming me so I would give in and give you a baby that neither of us want."

Raquel's onyx eyes widened in shock. She never knew that Alexander didn't want kids. She'd just assumed he put it off all this time because he wasn't ready.

"I want kids. I wanted kids with my husband. I never pretended to be anything, especially innocent. I never thought that swinging would help us. But I did think it was something you needed to get out of your system before we started a family." She shook her head in sadness. "However, I see that I was delusional to think this marriage was even worth saving. You don't want kids, you don't want me, and you definitely don't want this marriage. I was a fool, but not anymore."

⚜

IT HAD BEEN OVER TWO WEEKS SINCE RAQUEL AND ALEXANDER returned from their vacation. After their fight, Alexander moved into the guest room and they were barely speaking to one another. The school year had begun and Raquel was spending most of her days buried in schedules and enrollment forms, and her nights were spent drinking wine and wallowing in self-pity.

It was time for her to be a woman about her problems and talk to her husband. They couldn't continue ignoring each other and walking on egg shells. They were adults and their relationship was crumbling.

Raquel hesitantly knocked on the guest room door. She could hear Alexander speaking in hush tones, but she couldn't make out what he was saying.

"Just a minute." Raquel could hear the aggravation in his tone, and she almost turned around. The last thing she wanted was to have another argument.

However, before she could leave, the door swung open. Alexander's brown hair was disheveled and his face was covered with stubble. There were deep dark circles beneath his eyes and Raquel felt a pang of guilt at the look of her husband.

Obviously, he was suffering because of their argument just as much as she was. Instead of letting her thoughts welter, she should've been taking care of her husband. She'd given up on their marriage entirely too easy. She let lust cloud her judgment.

"Hey, baby. Are you okay?" Raquel reached for Alexander's rough jaw. She caressed his face lovingly, regretting all of the time they had spent fighting.

Alexander sighed as he pulled her into his body for a tight hug. Raquel hugged her husband back just as tight.

"I'm so sorry, baby. We should've never gone to that resort." Alexander's voice was full of regret, and Raquel felt the tension finally leave her body.

"No, we shouldn't have, but we can't take it back. What's done is done." Raquel responded, leaning back and looking into Alexander's eyes.

"Yes, I know. We can go to counseling. I know that was something you wanted to do in the past. I'll do whatever you want me to do as long as we can put this all behind us." The pleading look and tone wasn't like her husband, but maybe he could see how much this situation had hurt their marriage.

"I think counseling is definitely something we should look into. But first, why don't we sit down and have dinner and talk about what we really want and need out of this marriage." Raquel suggested, and Alexander nodded his head.

Raquel prepared a simple dinner of baked chicken and salad. When they sat down to eat, the air was thick with tension.

"I need you to forgive me for my transgressions at the resort. I know you, Raquel. You will hold this over my head for the rest of our lives." Alexander spoke hesitantly.

"I'll have to be honest with you, Alexander. I've been hurting for a long time, and it will take some time for me to forgive you. Hell, it will take time for me to forgive myself." Raquel responded truthfully.

"I understand. But this will never work if we don't forgive." Alexander's voice was pleading and Raquel nodded her agreement.

"What about kids?" She asked the question that had haunted her thoughts since their argument. If he really didn't want children, she needed to decide if that was a deal breaker for her. She didn't want to end up bitter and resentful.

Alexander sighed, "I think we should talk with the counselor about kids. I want us to both be open and in a safe place when we discuss our future."

Raquel didn't like the sound of that, but if speaking with a therapist would help her husband open up then that's what they would do.

"Okay, I'll make an appointment."

After they put away the dishes, they shared a bed for the first time since returning from vacation. Although the tension had somewhat decreased, it was still hovering over them like a dark cloud.

They didn't make love that night or the many nights after. For two weeks, they merely existed, only talking about mundane things like work. They were going through the motions and it was killing Raquel.

⚜

RAQUEL SAT AT HER DESK TRYING DESPERATELY TO CONCENTRATE. She had gone over the same student enrollment application several times and she still had no idea how to get the young lady into the necessary classes for graduation. A knock on the door garnered Raquel's attention.

"Come in."

"Mrs. Vincent, did you finish the new enrollment forms?" Jana Strauss, the school principal and Raquel's boss asked as she sauntered in with a look of superiority. Her nose was upturned and her hazel eyes twinkled with maliciousness.

Jana Strauss was new to the school but not the district. She and Raquel had crossed paths several times in the past for district meetings and holiday celebrations. However, the other woman didn't seem to become unreasonably nasty until she received the promotion to principal.

Raquel did her best not to scowl at the other woman. Ms. Strauss was a pain in the ass, and she thought hounding her staff was a way for them to respect her. She tried to rule with fear, but she was really a lack luster principal with no leadership skills what-so-ever.

"Ms. Strauss, I'm not sure how your last school operated, but new enrollment procedures take at least a week. These forms were given to me today. There's no possible way they would be finished."

"Well, I was told you were the veteran counselor, so completing them wouldn't be an issue for you." The woman smirked.

Raquel smiled holding back her ire. She knew the woman's type. If she couldn't intimidate, she would do her best to make the work environment uncomfortable. Raquel had plenty of recent experiences with being uncomfortable, so she wasn't bothered. And a short rotund bitch with a nasty attitude couldn't intimidate her either.

"I'm sure with your limited experience as an actual principal and not an assistant would make you think veteran means magician. I assure you, ma'am it does not. I'm also sure you are well aware the process takes at least a week, not a couple of hours. So, no. The enrollment forms are not completed."

The other woman's lips turned up in a sneer as she tossed her long brunette locks over her shoulder. "I may not have experience as a principal, but..."

Raquel held up her hand as her phone began to ring, cutting off the self-righteous spiel.

"Hello, this is Mrs. Vincent. Can you hold for one moment please?" Raquel placed her hand over the receiver before addressing her principal once more.

"I'm sorry, Ms. Strauss. This is the help desk returning my call about the enrollment forms. I'll need to take this, so if you'll excuse me." Raquel smiled sweetly as she effectively dismissed the other woman.

Ms. Strauss threw her one last dirty look before storming out of the office. Raquel continued with the call, but her mind was elsewhere. She knew that Jana Strauss was going to be an even bigger issue now that they'd had words.

"One more freaking thing I didn't need." Raquel sighed out loud as she gathered her things to leave. At least she would get to talk about her marital issues when she and Alexander had their first visit with Dr. Oliver.

When she arrived at the office, Alexander was already waiting with the doctor. He looked anxious, which in turn made Raquel nervous. She had to make sure to give herself an internal pep talk.

As they began the session, the uneasy feelings increased tenfold. Alexander's jumpy disposition didn't help either.

"So who would like to start?" Dr. Oliver asked, looking between the two of them.

"I will." Alexander volunteered. He hadn't made eye contact with Raquel since she walked in, and he was still avoiding looking at her.

"Okay, where would you like to begin?" The doctor's tone was soothing and the look on her light brown face was nonjudgmental.

"I don't think my wife will ever forgive me for suggesting we try..."

Alexander hesitated, "swinging." His voice was low and regretful, but Raquel shook her head before he could continue.

"That's not true. It will just take time. I can forgive you, Alexander." Raquel didn't know if she was trying to convince him or herself. But they'd come this far, and giving up wasn't something she wanted to do.

Alexander shook his head as he finally looked her in her eyes. "It is true. We haven't been intimate since we got back from the resort."

"I told you it would take time for me to forgive you. I can't just have sex with you…"

"You 'just' had sex with, Noah!" Alexander interrupted her with a shout.

"Okay, guys. Let's calm down. I know emotions are running high, but shouting at one another isn't communicating." Dr. Oliver's words helped them to calm down, but Raquel was still feeling irritated by her husband's attitude.

"So, you want me to forgive you, but you want to throw Noah in my face every chance you get." Raquel squinted her eyes in disgust.

"This is a place for us to be honest, right? You want to act like you're the only one that has something to forgive. You've been acting like sex with me is a chore for years now." Alexander spat angrily.

"That's not true!"

"It is true! That's why I made an appointment to have a vasectomy. If my wife isn't ever in the mood now, what would happen once we had kids? No! Fuck that! I'm not having kids!" Alexander's chest was moving as if he'd just finished a marathon. Raquel could see the truth in his eyes, he'd never planned on having children with her.

"A vasectomy?" Raquel whispered the two words laced with hurt.

"I told you I didn't want children, Raquel. But, you never listen to me." Alexander was no longer shouting but the damage had been done.

"You only told me that you didn't want kids four weeks ago. We've been married for over a decade."

"When I said I wasn't ready, you ignored me. You continued to hound me every chance you got." The snarl was back on his face.

"Hound you?" Raquel looked at him with disbelieving eyes.

"It sounds like we are at an impasse. You guys have a lot of anger toward one another, and we have to learn how to communicate without blaming and shouting. We should end the discussion for now." Dr. Oliver interrupted.

"No, we are not at an impasse. We are at the end. I want a divorce." Raquel's limit had been reached. This marriage was over.

What's done is done.

10

UP TO NO GOOD

"Hey, babe, I'm going out for a little while with Lucy. I'll be back later on." Giselle kissed Noah on the cheek as she quickly left their house.

Noah nodded without saying anything. Since they had been home from their vacation, Giselle had been acting strange. She had always been a free spirit and walked to the beat of her own drum, which was what Noah loved about her. But lately, she had been secretive and guarded.

Giselle had been sneaking around, taking whispered phone calls, and disappearing often. The only thing Noah asked of his wife was for her to communicate with him. All she had to do was tell him what she wanted, and he would move heaven and earth to get it for her. And because he had proven to her time and time again that she could have anything, there was no need for her behavior.

Normally, he would be too busy to notice his wife's odd behavior, but his time with Raquel had changed him. Noah saw how desperate a woman could be for love, and he didn't want his wife to ever feel like he didn't love her. And although he spoiled Giselle with material things, Noah hardly ever had time to spend with her. So he decided to change that, but it seemed his wife had other ideas.

Noah stalked in his home office and turned on his computer. He was a man who didn't like secrets. As a matter of fact, he made a career out of solving mysteries.

The screen lit up with his company logo and name, *Noah Palmer Investigations*. He quickly logged into the tracking device app he had on all of their cars and phones. It only took him a few minutes to see that his wife was at a hotel across town.

"Just what the fuck I thought." Noah frowned at the location. He had no idea why Giselle decided to lie to him after everything they had been through. There was no reason for her to run off and sneak around. They were always open and honest until now.

Noah wasn't the jealous husband type, but lying and hiding shit wasn't for him. He was going to confront Giselle as soon as he found out what the hell she was up to. So the first thing he needed to do was a little recon.

The drive over to the Wilkerson Hotel was a short one. Noah didn't let his mind wander to what if's and hypotheticals. He would get to the bottom of Giselle's duplicity and go from there.

Noah parked his car across the street and waited. It wouldn't be a smart move to go rushing into the hotel looking for his wife. She'd been gone for at least forty-five minutes. Hell, she could be anywhere in the hotel.

As Noah waited, he couldn't help but see the irony in his situation. When he first started his business, a lot of his time was spent investigating cheating spouses. He had eventually grown into a more sophisticated operation, dealing with identity theft, check and credit card fraud, and embezzlement.

However, every now and then he would go back to his roots and work a cheating spouse case for a friend or an acquaintance.

He waited for over a half an hour before he saw Giselle coming out of the hotel. Noah sat up in his seat as he watched his wife and a slender woman with platinum blond hair talking.

Since Giselle said she would be with Lucy, a petite black woman with jet black hair, Noah was confused about who the other woman was, and why his wife would lie to him. The whole thing felt suspicious and he absolutely hated the feeling.

He watched the two women walk into the adjacent parking lot and get into their vehicles. Once Giselle pulled away, Noah followed the other the woman. The black Mercedes coupe pulled out and headed toward an even more upscale part of town than where the hotel was located. Noah continued to tail the woman at a safe distance, but when she pulled into a secure garage, he had to end his pursuit.

Following the woman hadn't been a total bust because he was able to get her license plate number. At least with that bit of information he could try to trace down who the car belonged to and who the woman was.

Noah hit the phone icon on the steering wheel, and it rang once before the call was connected.

"What can I do for you, Mr. Palmer?"

"Hey, Manny. I need you to run a plate for me. I'm not at my desk." Noah could always count on Manny Palacio, his right hand man, to get any job done.

"No problem. Go ahead, boss." Manny responded without hesitation.

Noah read off the plate number and told Manny to make it a priority. It could take a few minutes to a few hours to get the information he needed. The plates could be fake, or unregistered, or registered incorrectly. There was a multitude of reasons why the license plate could lead to nowhere, but hopefully, Manny could work his magic.

"I'll have something for you in a few hours. Anything else, chief?" Manny questioned as his typing echoed in the background.

"Nah, but be sure to call me as soon as you find somethin' out."

"Sure thing." Manny answered still typing away.

Noah disconnected the call knowing that the task was in good hands, but he still couldn't help but wonder what the hell his wife was doing. Giselle was always doing things to get his attention, but he was certain that this time it wasn't about her attention seeking behavior. She was never sneaky and lying wasn't really her style.

Noah didn't believe Giselle was cheating on him with another woman because she would never do that. They might have been in the swinging life style and even did partner swaps, but Giselle was adamant about never being with another woman.

No, his wife wasn't cheating with the blond woman, but she was definitely up to something.

ॐ

GISELLE

GISELLE SAUNTERED INTO THE HOTEL'S BAR WITH CONFIDENCE. THE male attention she always received was on form. Every man she walked past gave her a heated look and she loved every minute of it.

Being with Noah all of these years had been stifling her natural urges. She did her best to be the perfect housewife, but it just wasn't what she wanted.

When she married Noah, she'd thought she'd hit the proverbial jackpot. He was handsome, straight, and rich! But he was also boring as all hell. When she introduced him to swinging, she figured that would solve her need for attention, but it didn't.

Giselle finally came to the realization that it wasn't just the attention from men, it was the thrill of doing something forbidden.

Giselle had always been impulsive even from an early age, and doing what she wanted was something that she'd always done. So, having to walk the straight and narrow with Noah was daunting. She was a person who needed more than a little spice to be excited, and for a while swinging was helpful but she needed more.

"You sure are fancy, nowadays. Must be nice." Giselle would ignore the snarky tone from the other woman. Besides, she needed to play nice.

"A lot of things have changed. But I was always fancy." Giselle winked before she sat down.

The other woman chuckled before sipping her beer.

"We promised one another we'd get out the game once we got out. What the hell were you thinking, Aundrea?" Giselle cut straight to the chase.

"We all aren't lucky enough to marry some rich dude. I had to do what I had to do to survive." Aundrea shrugged her shoulders nonchalantly. "So yeah, I ran into some trouble a few years back. A mark had more influence and power than I gave him credit for. And I had to do a bid." Aundrea acted like going to prison was no big deal. But Giselle knew prison was definitely a big deal.

"I told you that scamming men wasn't the way to go after we got caught. We were on too many radars." Giselle scolded.

"We were teenagers; our records were sealed and nobody knew about what we did! I was doing just fine."

Giselle shook her head before flipping her long blond hair over her shoulder. "Yeah, you were doing just fine, until you weren't. You never listen. But you will this time because I have the perfect plan, and you are the perfect person. And when it's all said and done, you'll never have to scam again."

NOAH

Later that night, Giselle continued to act strange. Noah observed her as she paced back and forth in their living room. She constantly checked her cell phone and she was watching the window like she was waiting on someone.

"Lookin' for somebody?" Noah didn't miss the way Giselle nearly jumped out of her skin.

"Oh my goodness! I didn't hear you come in, baby." Giselle clutched her chest as her face broke into a seductive smile. Noah arched a brow at his wife. She would always play the sultry southern belle when she wanted to distract him.

"So, who are you lookin' for?" Noah asked again. Giselle's fake smile dropped from her face as she turned her back to him.

"I don't know what you're talking about. I'm not looking for anybody." She waved her hand before she moved toward the recliner and sat down.

Giselle fidgeted with her phone before grabbing the remote and turning on the television. Noah continued to watch her closely, his suspicions growing with each of her denials. He knew that he'd have to come with evidence before she would tell him what was going on, so he would have to wait to confront her.

"So how is Lucy?" Noah asked.

Giselle's eyes widened and she swallowed hard before looking away. Noah watched her try to think of an answer, and he wanted to just put her out of her misery and tell her he knew she wasn't with Lucy like she had claimed. But he wouldn't.

"Lucy's Lucy. You know how she is." Giselle answered. She picked up the remote again and started flipping through the channels.

"Hmm. Well, she called the house looking for you earlier. She said she'd called your cell, but you didn't answer."

"No telling about Lucy. I'll give her call." Giselle hopped up and left the room so fast, Noah could've sworn she left a cloud a smoke in her wake.

"Well, that conversation went nowhere." Noah shook his head.

He thought of Raquel and how easy it was for him to talk to her. Even though their time together was brief, she was someone who wasn't far from his thoughts. She was sweet, kind, and loving. After she relaxed, she was a lot of fun and had a killer sense of humor. Giselle was all about herself, and even though that had always been the case, it bothered the hell out of him now.

Noah wanted to have a connection to his wife again. He wanted to be able to laugh, joke, and relax with her like he'd done with a total stranger. He wanted to love and feel loved. But he didn't have either of those things.

Although it was late, Noah checked his phone to see if Manny had left a message. It seemed the woman was harder to find than he'd expected. The car was a rental and Manny would have to hack into a few difficult systems before he could get to the rental agreement.

Noah was hoping it would be a simple hack, but when he didn't see any missed or new messages he knew that it would take longer than he thought.

He sighed in frustration. Noah wasn't one for regrets, but his life had been just fine before this last vacation. Meeting Raquel had opened his eyes to things that he wished could've stayed hidden.

That night when he went to bed, Giselle was already snoring softly on her side. She had disappeared into their bedroom and never made it back to the living room to continue their talk. It was obvious she was doing her best to avoid any and all conversation about what she was doing that day.

Noah stayed awake looking at the ceiling and thinking about his life. He didn't think he would be here at his age. He was thirty-nine, lying in bed wondering what his wife was doing and where she was going. Second guessing his decisions and questioning if he was actually happy.

Once, he had thought he was living his best life. Swinging was something he enjoyed because he was able to sleep with beautiful women without his marriage ending in divorce. His wife was happy and that was all he'd ever wanted. But now, he wanted more.

🦋

THE NEXT MORNING, GISELLE WAS ALREADY GONE WHEN NOAH woke up. She was usually at the gym or running, at least that was what she would tell him.

Noah wasn't the type of man to sit around and sulk. He also wouldn't twiddle his thumbs while his wife snuck around lying. If he found out Giselle was having an affair, then their marriage would be done.

Noah made it perfectly clear he wouldn't tolerate dishonesty. Part of their agreement in their relationship had always been they'd been open and honest with one another. They started swinging after they talked and agreed.

Giselle knew if she wanted out of their marriage all she had to do was say so. It would hurt, but Noah was not the type of guy who wanted to be with someone for the sake of not being alone. His wife also knew if he ever caught her cheating, he would leave her ass with nothing and without a second thought.

Noah gave Giselle whatever she wanted whenever she wanted, but they had an ironclad prenup. And if Giselle broke the agreement she would leave with nothing. So Noah couldn't understand why a woman who stood to lose millions of dollars and had a husband that spoiled her rotten would take the risk.

After taking a shower, Noah got dressed and grabbed breakfast. He decided he would be too distracted to work from home, so he headed to the office.

"Hey, Mr. Palmer. I got the rental agreement for the car." Manny handed the paperwork over as soon as Noah stepped foot inside the door.

Noah nodded. "I knew I could count on you."

Noah waited until he got into his office before opening up the folder with the forms. As he scanned the information, the mystery only grew. Once he read the name of the renter, he knew for sure his wife was up to no good.

"Giselle Palmer, renter. What the hell are you up to?"

11

COMING TO TERMS

ALEXANDER "I told you not to call me at this time of day. I'm at home and Raquel could be home any minute now."

"You told me a lot of things, Alexander! What happened to getting a divorce?"

"I told you baby," Alexander's voice was soothing, "Raquel refuses to get a divorce. She's determined to make us stay together and have kids. She wants to go to counseling."

"What!" Her voice was shrill and Alexander rolled his eyes. The woman was so gullible it was pathetic. She would believe any and everything he said.

"Calm down. I have a plan and it won't matter what Raquel wants. Especially if she's dead."

"As long as we're together I'll do whatever it takes."

"Perfect!"

RAQUEL WAS STILL IN SHOCK BECAUSE OF ALEXANDER'S PLANS TO GET a vasectomy without telling her. His revelation opened her eyes to a man she didn't know.

Raquel always wanted a family and Alexander had known that, but instead of being honest and telling her he didn't want kids, he kept her dangling on a string with a promise he had no intentions on keeping.

He was right about one thing; she couldn't forgive him. She had wasted fifteen years of her life with a selfish man that gave her no consideration. Raquel was done. Alexander had moved out and she was trying to move on, but it was difficult.

She had to start her life over, which logically wasn't a bad thing, but she couldn't help but feel bad. The main reason she had gone to the swinger's resort was so she could *fix* her marriage and not end up a thirty-seven-year-old divorcée. However, saving her marriage didn't seem to be in the cards.

Thinking back over it all, Raquel had known it would never work between them. Swinging wasn't ever something she even considered, and something she should've never done. However, she'd done it. But what had made her a fool was she didn't want to see what was right in front of her.

No man would ever trade getting new booty for a child. What sane man would propose that he'd give his wife the kids she wanted in exchange for her permission to sleep with other women? Raquel had to shake her head at how dumb she had acted. Deep down she'd known Alexander didn't want children, but she was being too stubborn to admit it.

Raquel rubbed her temples as she tried to keep a migraine from coming. She'd been having them more often with all the nonsense she had been dealing with. On top of her relationship woes, her principal had been acting like a grade-A psychopath.

Ever since they'd exchanged words, Ms. Strauss made it her mission to try to make Raquel miserable. Every new student was given to Raquel no matter what level they were in because Raquel had the least amount of students in her assigned grade. Raquel was given every assignment and paperwork procedure for the entire school. When she mentioned to the principal the system they had in place, Ms. Strauss exploded saying, she was the boss and Raquel could do what she said or find another job.

Raquel turned her in for harassment and creating a hostile working environment. And because Raquel took meticulous notes and recorded some of Strauss' outbursts, the principal was being investigated.

However, the school system was always slow to remove administrators, so Raquel still had to see the woman nearly every day. Ms. Strauss kept her distance, but she made it known that she didn't like Raquel and made every move possible to undermine her work.

"Hey, Mrs. Vincent. You got a minute for an old friend?"

Raquel looked up and smiled as she rose from her desk. Patrice Elliot was one of her dearest friends. The woman could light up any room with her personality and she was right on time because Raquel needed a friend more than ever.

"Well, if it isn't Mrs. Elliot." Raquel and Patrice embraced each other tightly. "You look great! Coming in here glowing and stuff. I guess that second honeymoon was just what you needed."

"Girl, after being married for ten years and all the shit we've been through, a second honeymoon was exactly what we needed."

"I hear you." Raquel's smile faltered just a little. She didn't begrudge her friend's happiness, but she was sad that her own vacation turned out so differently.

"So, do you have a few minutes to spare? Maybe we can go to lunch." Patrice looked at her watch at the same time Raquel looked down at hers.

"Actually, I have a doctor's appointment. But how about we meet for dinner?" Raquel questioned. She was honestly tired of eating alone so she could use the company.

"Okay, that will work. Deaton is catching up on clients anyway, so he won't miss me tonight." Patrice smiled saucily.

Raquel laughed because Patrice's husband, Deaton, was known for being so overprotective of his wife that he had hired a bodyguard when he left town for more than one night. So he would definitely "miss" her if she weren't around.

"I'm sure Deaton would say different." Raquel responded, still laughing.

They made plans to catch up later on that evening and Raquel finished out the rest of her day. She was anxious about speaking with Dr. Oliver on her own. It was supposed to be a couple's session, but Raquel decided that working on herself was more important.

As she finished up her paperwork and turned off her computer, she heard voices outside of her office. Raquel recognized the annoying screeching right away and the automatic response to roll her eyes couldn't be contained.

"I'm so glad I'm leaving." Raquel mumbled as she grabbed her purse and headed toward the door.

When she turned to lock her office door, it seemed the voices had gotten closer.

"Are you leaving for the day?" Ms. Strauss had her hand on her hips as she tapped the floor with her pointy toed shoes. Raquel wanted to laugh at the irony of the woman dressing like a witch.

"Yes." It was better if Raquel left little to no room for misunderstandings. She learned direct yes or no answers was the best way to deal with the unreasonable woman.

"I didn't approve that. Leaving early without approval is a write up." She smirked and Raquel simply smiled.

"I got approval from the counseling director because that's who I directly report to now." Raquel kept the bite out of her voice, but she knew the meaning behind her words wasn't lost on Ms. Strauss. Jana was under investigation and because of that, none of the counseling department reported directly to her.

"I still should've been notified." She sneered.

Raquel shrugged. "I did my part, so it's above me now. You have a good rest of your day."

RAQUEL SIPPED A GLASS OF WINE AS SHE LOOKED OVER THE MENU. Even though it was a Friday evening, she still wanted to take it easy on the drinking. Her migraine had gone away, but she didn't want a hangover either.

"Hey, lady. Sorry I'm late. Deaton wanted some special time before

I could leave." Patrice leaned over and gave Raquel a hug as she moved her eyebrows up and down suggestively.

The women shared a laugh before settling into conversation. It had been a while since they had gotten together, and it was good to catch up. Raquel didn't have a lot of friends, but the ones she did have were close. However, Patrice would be the first friend Raquel would tell about her separation from Alexander.

"So, how was your vacation? You really do look rejuvenated." Raquel complimented.

"Well, hell, you act like a sista was looking raggedy." Patrice laughed.

"No. Of course, you always look slayed. But you have this relaxed aura around you that wasn't there before."

"Thank you. I was just kidding." Patrice laughed as she swatted her hand in Raquel's direction. "I know I needed a break. I was tired and my loving husband noticed."

"That's good. I'm glad you got some rest." Raquel nodded. She didn't want to be envious of her friend's *loving husband*, but the pang in her chest was immediate.

She stuffed the feeling down and focused on the positive. Dr. Oliver told her it was okay to have negative thoughts as long as she didn't wallow in them. She needed to address them and move on to the positive.

"I'm talking all about my get away, but how was your trip to Jamaica?" Patrice asked.

Raquel could feel the tears well up in her eyes. "Alexander and I are separated. Going to Jamaica opened my eyes to things I ignored for a long time." Raquel shook her head as the tears began to fall. "I was stupid and now I have to face the decisions I made."

"Oh, honey, I'm so sorry. I had no idea you were going through any of this. Why didn't you tell me?" Patrice took her hand and gave her a tissue.

Raquel wiped her eyes and took a deep breath, trying to get herself together. "I suppose I thought if I said it out loud and people knew then it would be real. But it's real whether I say it or not. Alexander is gone. He moved into an apartment and we've had little to no contact in three weeks."

"Well, hell. I thought you guys were doing well." Patrice's face was filled with confusion and Raquel couldn't blame her friend. Her and Alexander always put on a good show, so nobody would ever guess they were having marital issues.

Raquel shrugged. "I don't think we've been doing well for a few years now. I just didn't want to admit it."

"Well, sweetie, you know that Deaton and I are always here for you. We've had our own trials and tribulations, so I may not know exactly what you're going through, but I've had my share of issues."

Raquel nodded. "Thank you. I really needed to hear that."

The two friends continued to discuss their problems before moving onto lighter topics. Raquel was glad to have a friend she could confide in without worry of judgment. Once she left the restaurant, she felt ten times better. Although Raquel had spoken to Dr. Oliver, it was nothing like speaking to a loved one who gave their understanding.

The whole conversation made her think of Noah. He was so laid back and accepting. He never judged her for being uptight or out of her element. Noah just simply steered her into having more fun. Raquel could appreciate all he had done for her. He had helped her accept things and go with the flow, and that was definitely a lesson she needed to apply in her current state.

"I can do this. I have no choice but to do this. I would rather start over than live in misery." Raquel spoke the words out loud. If she said them enough maybe she would start to believe them.

As Raquel drove along trying to think positively, her phone rang and the Bluetooth automatically connected before she had a chance to decline the call.

"Hello? Raquel?" Alexander's voice came through loud and clear.

Raquel immediately wanted to hang up. But she wouldn't. Being mature and facing her husband was something Dr. Oliver told her she would need to do eventually.

"Hello. What do you need?" Raquel wouldn't hang up, but that didn't mean she had to be nice. She was still salty about him lying to her for all those years, and it would take her quite some time to get over it.

His loud sigh came through the car speakers as if he were sitting right next to her. "Raquel, I just wanted to hear your voice. Maybe we could sit down and talk about things since we didn't have our couple's counseling session."

"We're not a couple anymore, so we don't need sessions together. I've already explained that to you and you accepted it. You lied to me for years, Alexander. Do you think I'm going to just get over that?" Raquel's voice was loud and irritated.

"I didn't lie to you, Raquel." Alexander huffed.

"Is it crack? Is that the drug you're on? Because I know for sure you confessed in our first and only session you never wanted children, and you've even planned to have a vasectomy behind my back! You know you made me believe we wanted the same things!" Raquel yelled into the phone. She couldn't keep her cool in the face of his blatant arrogance. *The audacity.*

"Raquel, don't be foolish. Just because I may have wanted children in the past doesn't mean I can't change my mind. I was just waiting to make sure we were stable before we made such a big decision, and the longer we waited, I began to realize we didn't need children."

Those were the exact words he had fed her for years. *"Wait until we're stable."* They both were gainfully employed and together they had a generous six figure income. They were plenty stable, and Alexander was full of shit. He knew all along he didn't want kids. Raquel might have played the fool before, but she refused to continue to do so.

"We're certainly unstable now, aren't we? Listen, you knew all I ever wanted was my own family, and you denied me of that. The only thing left to talk about is *divorce.*"

"You can't mean that, Raquel. You're upset right now and I get it. But we've been together too long for you to just walk away."

"We've been together too long for you to continue to lie to me!" Raquel hated that Alexander was discounting her feelings.

"If you try to get alimony, I will fight you. I'm not the only guilty party in this relationship. It takes two people to make a marriage fail."

Alexander's threat was loud and clear. Alimony, was why he was fighting the divorce idea not love.

Raquel was about to give him a piece of her mind, but all of a sudden, there was a high pitch squeal of tires and headlights that shined directly into her eyes. She tried to slam on her brakes, but the car wasn't slowing down. Raquel swerved to miss the oncoming driver, but it was too late.

Before she knew it, the car took flight through the air. She felt like a rag doll as her body flung from side to side. The seatbelt was restraining her from going through the windshield. It tightened across her chest and kept her clamped in place.

When the airbag deployed, it hit Raquel directly in her face. *I don't want to die,* flittered across her mind before everything went black.

❧ 12 ❧

CONSEQUENCES

Noah still hadn't figured out the identity of the blond mystery woman Giselle had met with, but the rental car had been returned and his wife had stopped acting suspicious. So he decided to just let it go for the time being. Maybe his wife was just helping out a friend. There was really no telling what she was up to, and Noah figured he would focus on the positive things about his wife and move on.

When the phone rang, Noah smiled and picked it up right away.

"Hey, darlin." Noah's deep voice carried over the line.

"Hi, baby. What are you up to?" Giselle's tone was sultry, so Noah knew she wanted something.

"Just doin' some work. What about you? Do you have any plans for the day?" Noah asked, keeping the conversation light.

Giselle didn't call him during the day that often, and he liked the idea of his wife showing interest in his day.

"Oh you know, same ole same. I wanted to call and reschedule our dinner plans for tonight. I'm going to be late helping Julie and Penelope with the charity event."

"No problem, darlin'. Just be sure to let me know when you're on the way home so I won't worry."

"Oh, well, I may spend the night downtown with Penelope if it gets too late. You know I don't like to drive by myself at night."

"Alright. Just let me know either way." Noah responded with a frown.

"Okay, I will. Talk to you later. Bye." Giselle disconnected the call before he could respond.

He continued to frown down at the phone. Noah knew she was buttering him up for something by the tone of her voice. Giselle was a party girl in the past, and sometimes when she was hanging out with her friends, she forgot she was a thirty-eight-year-old married woman and not a twenty-two-year-old socialite.

However, Noah wasn't going to police his wife's behavior because she was a grown woman. And as long as she respected their agreement, he had nothing to say.

After their phone call, Noah got back to work. He had several cases that needed his attention, and although he promised himself he would be more attentive to his wife, he still needed to work.

As the day went on and Noah was working hard at his desk, he received a toll tag notification on his email that caught his attention. He would've ignored it, but because it had a flashing red exclamation point next to it, Noah stopped to take care of the alert. It turned out to be an expired credit card on his account. However, when he read the details of the notification, he realized letting go of his suspicions when it came to his wife was the wrong thing to do.

Noah examined the recent transactions with a furrowed brow. His square jaw was held tight as he ground his teeth with narrowed eyes. His suspicions were confirmed and it was right there in front of him in black and white.

Giselle had been making numerous road trips to Dallas, Texas. She had never even mention leaving town. And although Dallas was only about three hours from their hometown of Austin, neither of them had close friends or family there. And because Giselle was a housewife, she didn't have any business dealings or work related ventures in Dallas either.

It could've had something to do with the charity she volunteered for, but why would she keep her trips a secret? There were a lot of things not adding up, and it was beyond time to get to the bottom of what was going on.

"Who the hell is in Dallas?" Before the words were completely out of his mouth, Raquel's beautiful onyx eyes and bright smile flashed in his mind. Noah shook his head to rid himself of the image.

Raquel lived in Dallas *with her husband,* Noah amended as an afterthought. It had been close to three months since he'd seen her last, and as hard as he'd tried not to think about her, she still invaded his thoughts from time to time.

Noah ran his hand through his hair to regain his focus. And once he continued to review the toll account, Noah quickly recovered his concentration. He saw that Giselle had been driving to Dallas three to four times a month for at least six months.

This wasn't something Noah could simply ignore. He was an investigator by nature and by profession. To leave Giselle's obvious duplicity unchecked would be idiotic, so he once again logged into the system for the tracking device on her car.

After about an hour, Noah was able to get the exact locations Giselle had visited in Dallas. The more information he discovered, the madder he got. After running the addresses, it was clear that Giselle had played him for a fool.

"What the fuck is going on with my life right now?" Noah pounded his fist against the desk in anger.

It was apparent Giselle thought because she'd gotten away with her lies for so long that she would continue getting away with them. Noah was so busy with his career and pleasing her that he'd never suspected anything was off.

Giselle paid all of the household bills, and if it weren't for the email notification, Noah would've never known anything was amiss. It was a good thing she didn't know about the tracking devices on the cars.

Noah was going to tell her, but he knew that she would throw a fit and he saw it as a necessary security precaution. Even though the cars were equipped with the latest edition GPS systems, Manny would've had to hack all kinds of structures if they didn't have their own tracking devices, so Noah thought it was easier to have his own systems in place. He was right.

With all the evidence piled in his face, Noah had a few choices to make. He could either confront Giselle with what he already had, he could wait to see what she would do next, or he could dig even deeper and get everything he needed for an undisputed divorce.

Noah decided on the latter. It was time he took a trip to Dallas.

※

THE THREE HOUR RIDE TO DALLAS WAS SPENT IN CONTEMPLATION. Noah didn't know what the hell he would be walking into, and even though his life was slowly crumbling, he was glad to finally have some clarity.

He didn't want to cause any trouble, and in Texas if you were trespassing on somebody's property, the owner had a right to shoot you. So Noah found himself in a very precarious situation.

Once he arrived in Dallas, he checked into a hotel. It was late and he wanted to get some rest and clear his head. He'd left Giselle a message letting her know he had to leave town for a case, so she wouldn't be looking for him in case she decided to come home. Noah half expected to find her in Dallas, but the device on her car showed it parked at Penelope's downtown apartment, so at least she hadn't lied about that.

Noah tossed and turned for most of the night, resulting in a fitful night's sleep. Even though he was considered a no nonsense, blunt, rough and tumble guy, he was still a man who loved his wife. He had feelings just like anyone else.

People would often judge their life style as swingers, but it was nobody's business what a married couple agreed upon. When Noah and Giselle decided to become swingers, it would only happen on vacation and with the other person's knowledge. Cheating was still cheating even in a swinger's relationship.

If your partner wasn't privy to your outside activities, and consent hadn't been granted, it was *cheating*. Noah and Giselle agreed to that and as crazy as it may sound, it had even been added to their prenup.

With a heart filled with dread, Noah began his journey to the address where Giselle's car was tracked. The neighborhood was nice and quiet with manicured lawns and gardens. He could definitely see a couple making a life for themselves there.

He pulled up and parked his car in the circular driveway. Even though it was early evening when people should've been off work, it didn't look like anyone was home. Noah got out of his car and headed toward the front door anyway.

Before he could knock however, an elderly woman with a short, gray bob and pale skin came from next door to greet him.

"Are you looking for the Vincent's?" Her eyebrows were high in question as curiosity covered her wrinkled face. It was something about the woman that made Noah think she was the neighborhood gossip.

"Uh, yeah. Raquel and Alexander. Are they home?" Noah didn't want to engage in too much conversation with the woman, but if she had information he would bear it.

"Oh no, honey. Are you a friend of theirs? Because somebody should've let you know already that Raquel was in a horrible car accident last night." The woman stepped closer and looked around as if somebody was watching them.

Noah couldn't help himself as he looked around too. His heart beat frantically at the news. The last thing he was expecting to hear was that Raquel was hurt.

"Apparently, somebody ran her off the road. Came right at her car head on when she swerved. Flipped the car and crashed. It was just awful." The woman told everything she knew without prompting. Noah wondered how she had so many details about the accident.

"Is she alright? What hospital is she in?" Noah tried to inject calm into his voice, but he could feel the panic.

The woman scratched at her chin and looked to the sky. "I believe she's at Taylor Medical. My grandson is an officer, and my scanner picked up the accident last night. I haven't had a chance to call Alexander yet. I didn't want to intrude."

For some reason, Noah didn't believe the woman, but he was thankful for her nosiness. At least now, he could go and check on Raquel.

"Thank you, Mrs. um..." Noah trailed off because the woman had told him everything but her name.

"Pitman. You're so welcome, young man." She smiled.

Noah nodded as he quickly got into his car. Hopefully, Raquel wasn't seriously injured. He hit the OnStar button as soon as he started his vehicle. He rattled off the hospital name quickly to get the directions he needed and set out to find out how Raquel was doing. The news of her accident had changed his plan entirely.

NOAH WANTED TO HAVE A CONVERSATION WITH ALEXANDER ABOUT Giselle. It was obvious that the two of them had met before they'd gone to Jamaica. As a matter of fact, it seemed they had known each other for at least six to eight months before the trip.

Noah didn't find that little tidbit of information out until after he'd arrived in Dallas. He had gone through Giselle's bank account and their joint account to find charges in Dallas, which led him to believe Giselle and Alexander had planned to meet up in Jamaica.

Noah still couldn't figure out why Alexander would want to drag his wife into his cheating or why Giselle hadn't just continued to lay low and have her affair. If it wasn't for her weird behavior, Noah never would've suspected anything. And if they'd never met Raquel and Alexander at the resort, he would've never suspected cheating was the reason behind her traveling to Dallas without him knowing.

None of it was adding up, but Noah's questions would have to wait until later. He needed to find Raquel's room. Hopefully, she was well enough to have visitors, and then maybe he wouldn't seem like a creeper showing up out of the blue unannounced.

When Noah made it to the hospital, he was able to use his charm and looks to find out a room number for Raquel. Fortunately for him, it was still visiting hours so he was allowed to go directly to her room.

It was extremely troublesome how easy it was for him to gain access to a patient without showing any identification what-so-ever. He shook his head at the lack of professionalism of the hospital. However, it helped to serve his purpose so he wouldn't complain too loud about the issues.

When Noah made it to Raquel's room, he could hear an argument taking place. Although he wanted to rush into the room to see what the hell was going on, he didn't. He stood by the door and eavesdropped. He could see through the small window in the door Raquel was in bed with Alexander standing beside her speaking to who he assumed was a doctor.

Alexander's face was beet red, and Raquel had tears streaming down her bruised cheeks.

"I'm sorry, but the test result is accurate. You are in your first trimester of pregnancy, ma'am." The doctor said and it made Noah stumble back. If Raquel was in her first trimester, then the baby could very well be *his*.

Before his brain could tell his body to leave, his feet led him inside the room.

"Noah? What are you doing here?" Raquel gasped, horror covering her face.

"Is it mine?" Noah asked, looking directly into Raquel's watery eyes.

13

STRIFE

"Is *what* yours? What the hell are you doing here?!" Alexander's yelling echoed throughout the room.

Although his shouting was unnecessary, Raquel wanted to know why Noah was there as well. Before she could ask, the two men started to argue loudly. Raquel was certain someone was going to call the police or she would die from embarrassment.

"Gentlemen, please lower your voices. You are in a hospital and Mrs. Vincent needs her rest." The doctor stated sternly. Although both men went silent, they stood staring daggers at one another.

"Dr. Patton, can you excuse us please?" Raquel's pleading voice was filled with mortification. She couldn't believe her life.

"No, problem. Push the call button if you need anything." The slender man nodded and left the room.

Raquel was absolutely humiliated. She couldn't believe this was happening to her. She didn't know what sins she had committed in her past life, but she prayed for forgiveness to the universe, God, her guardian angel, or whoever would listen.

As soon as the doctor shut the door behind him, a scowling red-faced Alexander turned his wrath toward her. Raquel couldn't really concentrate on what he was saying because of the shock of seeing

Noah again out of the nowhere. She also wanted to laugh at how worked up Alexander was at the situation. It seemed lately, his face was always red for some reason. *Serves his ass right.*

"Why would this man think this baby was his?" Alexander questioned. Raquel could hear the malice in his voice, but she couldn't bring herself to give a shit about his feelings. She was the one laid up in a hospital bed with a fractured leg and bruised clavicle. She didn't even want him to be there.

"Noah? What are you doing here?" Raquel repeated as she focused on him and completely ignored Alexander.

"Long story." Noah's crooked smile didn't reach his eyes and although their time together had been short, she could tell he was worried.

"We don't have time for your stories. You need to get the fuck out of this hospital room before I call security. My wife is hurt and we don't even know you." Alexander butted in unwelcomely.

"Alexander." Raquel called sharply to get his attention. When he turned to face her, she spoke slowly and calmly so he could understand. "I've already asked *you* to leave. And like you said, I'm hurt and I don't need the stress right now. Just go."

"I can't believe you want me to leave after the news we just got. I'm not leaving my pregnant wife here with a stranger." Alexander crossed his arms over his chest and frowned.

Raquel sighed. She really didn't want to deal with Alexander's petulance. Her body was sore, her head hurt, and she just received the most shocking news of her life. *I'm pregnant.*

"Listen, we both know I'm only legally your wife because you haven't signed the divorce papers, and let's not pretend you're happy about this pregnancy. You've told me numerous times that you don't want children. Now, I have asked you to leave. Noah being here doesn't change what I want. Please just go." Raquel stated firmly as she looked Alexander straight in his eyes.

Alexander's jaw was tightly clenched as he narrowed his brown eyes on her. If he thought he could intimidate her with his scowl, he was mistaken. Raquel continued to stare blankly back at him, practically daring him to say anything else. The only reason he was arguing to stay was because Noah had shown up.

"Raquel, we should talk about—"

"Just leave, man." Noah interrupted in a deep voice laced with pure malice, which served to make Raquel even more curious. She really wanted to know why and how Noah had shown up, but she wouldn't ask again until Alexander was gone.

"How dare you butt into our lives like this? Who the hell do you think you are?" Alexander stepped in Noah's direction and Raquel was afraid that she really would have to call security.

"You know exactly who the hell I am. I'm the man you 'chose' for your wife, right? Isn't that what you wanted us to believe?" Noah stated cryptically.

Alexander took a step back and visibly swallowed.

"I don't know what you're talking about." Alexander rushed out quickly.

"Although I drove two hundred miles to talk about this, it's neither the time nor the place right now. Let's not pretend you don't know what I'm talking about, though. I just needed some questions answered man to man. I didn't come to accuse you of anything, but I see now it was a wasted trip because you're worse than Giselle with your lies." Noah's words were a deep growl and Raquel wanted to know what in the hell was going on.

"What is he talking about, Alexander?" Raquel asked as she pushed the button on the bed so she could sit up higher.

Alexander shook his head as he turned to face her once more. "Nothing. He's not talking about anything important." Although he looked calm, Raquel had spent fifteen-years with him and she could see the panic in his gaze.

"So you're here to talk about Giselle?" Raquel turned her attention to Noah. His eyes connected with hers and she could see the truth staring her in the face.

"I'm here to talk about your health and the pregnancy. You know this baby could be mine, right?"

Raquel's mind flashed back to the one time they had gotten carried away, and in her grief and lust she hadn't worried about protection. She was automatically filled with dread and shame. She never would've even considered once she finally gotten pregnant it would be some scandalous "you are *not* the father" situation.

Raquel took a deep breath to rid herself of the negative thoughts. There was no turning back, and the decision was made. She got what she wanted which was a baby even if it was by unconventional means. And she was a strong woman who could figure anything out, so raising a baby by herself would be fine. Thousands of women did it every day, and she would be no exception.

"You cannot be serious! Raquel, please tell me this stranger is out of his mind and there is no possible way he could be the father!" Alexander's voice was loud once again and veins were popping out of his neck and forehead. He looked completely deranged.

"Lower your fucking voice." Noah took a step toward Alexander, but when he looked at Raquel he stopped.

"Alexander, Noah and I had sex around the time I got pregnant. You were there and you chose him. Babies come from *sex*." She said with exasperation.

"I can't believe this shit!" Alexander huffed.

"It was your idea, so believe it. Anyway, I didn't ask you to raise my child. The only thing I've asked you for was a divorce." Raquel responded.

She was tired of the show Alexander was putting on. They both knew whether the baby was his or not, he wasn't interested in having it. But Raquel wanted her child, and she was going to keep it. Circumstances be damned.

Raquel's head began pounding and the loud beeping of the heart monitor revealed her rising stress level. When the beeping became faster, and Raquel began to get nauseous, a tall nurse with kind, blue eyes stepped into the room.

"Mrs. Vincent, visiting hours are over, and it looks like you need to rest." The nurse smiled politely as she checked the monitors and Raquel's chart.

"Okay. You both need to leave." Raquel looked at Alexander and then Noah.

"I'm not leaving." Alexander protested.

However, Noah simply nodded as he made his way over to her bed. He kissed her forehead tenderly. "I'll see you tomorrow. Get some rest."

Raquel watched him leave the room before looking at Alexander with an arched brow. She needed some rest, and she definitely wouldn't be able to sleep peacefully with him hovering over her.

"Fine. I'll leave," he finally relented. "But I'll be back first thing tomorrow." Alexander didn't try to give Raquel a kiss since Noah left and the show was over. He stormed out of the room and she was thankful he was finally gone.

৩৫৩

GISELLE

WHEN THE PHONE RANG, GISELLE INSTANTLY SMILED. SHE HAD BEEN waiting on the call for what seemed like forever.

"What the fuck is your husband doing in Dallas, Giselle?" Giselle had never heard Alexander's voice so filled with venom. She thought this conversation would be in celebration of his wife's untimely death.

"What are you talking about? Noah is home where I left him." Giselle responded sharply.

"No, the fuck he is not!" Alexander yelled. "He's here in Dallas claiming *my* baby!"

"What the fuck are you saying? What baby?" Giselle could feel herself getting angrier by the second, and Alexander wasn't making a lick of sense.

"Raquel is in the hospital," Alexander paused but she read between the lines. *That bitch lived.*

"The doctor ran tests, and we found out she was pregnant. That's when *your* husband busted in the room claiming the baby and accusing me of sleeping with you."

"He doesn't know about us." Giselle was extremely confused now. She had been careful, and there was no way Noah knew about her and Alexander after all this time.

The humorless chuckle was loud on the other end of the phone. And Giselle instantly realized that all her plans would have to change.

"Oh, he definitely knows something. And if Raquel finds out we've been seeing each other over the last eight months she will definitely have cause for a divorce. We won't get a dime of money out of her if she's my ex-wife."

"Listen, you just continue to play doting regretful husband and father-to-be, and I will take care of the rest. I knew I shouldn't have left anything up to you in the first place. We shouldn't even be having this conversation because you *should* be grieving." Giselle's tone was hard and unforgiving.

She'd placed all of her bets on Alexander, and he had failed her. He was the perfect companion for her because he gave her attention, but he also loved the thrill of the forbidden. The main obstacles in their love was money and Raquel. If Raquel died, they would have plenty of money from her demise. But if she was alive, she would never go away and with her still in the picture their fun would be stifled. And Giselle hated being stifled.

"I'll take care of *it*, but you better tie up all your loose ends." Giselle warned before hanging up on Alexander, and making another call.

"Hello, Aundrea. I have another task for you, and this time it will be worth millions."

WHEN RAQUEL WOKE THE NEXT MORNING, SHE FINALLY HAD TIME to process all the information she'd been given the previous night. She moved her hand over her belly and smiled. She was pregnant. There was a life growing inside of her.

Right then and there, Raquel made a promise to herself and her unborn child that she would always protect and love him or her with all of her heart and soul.

She tried to sit up in her bed and an excruciating pain shot through the left side of her body making her wince in agony. That was when she remembered her predicament. Somebody ran her off the road and kept driving. If it wasn't for the good Samaritan who stopped and helped, she could've very well been stuck for hours in the ditch.

Although her leg was now hoisted up in a cast with bruises all over her body, Raquel was thankful. Thankful someone found her, thankful that she lived, and thankful the accident led to the discovery of her unknown pregnancy.

Because even though it was light, she'd had her period so Raquel didn't have a clue she was pregnant. It had never crossed her mind that she could be.

Raquel was completely lost in her thoughts when a light knock and a voice clearing garnered her attention. She faced the two strangers curiously.

"Mrs. Vincent?" The black woman had smooth brown skin and light brown eyes that held a hint of concern. The huge man with her looked like he could be her bodyguard. His imposing height and dark gaze gave off an air of intimidation.

"Yes, I'm Mrs. Vincent." Raquel responded cautiously.

"I'm Detective Garner and this is my partner, Detective Witt." The man nodded his greeting, but he didn't speak.

"Nice to meet you. Uh, can I help you with something?" Raquel asked confused.

"Yes, we wanted to know if you remember anything about your accident?" Detective Garner asked, taking out a pen and a small pad.

"Um, not much. I remember seeing headlights and then everything went black." Raquel answered, still confused as to why two detectives were asking her questions. Alexander told her the police on the scene said it was an accident, another driver had mistakenly drifted into oncoming traffic.

The person didn't hit Raquel, although he or she didn't stop to render aide either. But Raquel didn't think the authorities assigned detectives to those types of traffic violation.

"Did you try to hit your brakes when you saw the headlights?"

"Uh, yeah, I *think* I did." Raquel furrowed her brows as she tried to recall the memory. "Yes, I definitely hit the brakes, but it felt like I was pushing the petal to the floor and the car wasn't slowing down. That was when I swerved to get out of the way of the other car."

The detectives exchanged a look, which Raquel couldn't decipher before detective Garner continued her questioning. Once she was finished, Raquel was even more confused.

"Why are you asking me these questions?" Raquel cut to the chase.

"Ma'am, we don't think your car wreck was an accident." The detective responded slowly.

"Wait. What do you mean it wasn't an accident?"

"Your brake line was cut on your car, which was why you couldn't stop. Severed brake lines don't equal an accident." Detective Witt finally spoke. His tone wasn't as sympathetic as his partner's, but Raquel appreciated his straight to the point manner.

"Is there anyone who wants to hurt you?" Detective Garner asked.

"My wife, Giselle Palmer." Noah's deep voice came from the door.

"May I ask who you are, sir?"

"I'm Noah Palmer, a, uh, friend of Raquel's," Noah responded, looking over at her. Raquel shrugged, a friend was a better description than potential baby daddy who wasn't her husband.

"Why would you suspect your wife of having anything to do with Mrs. Vincent's accident?" Detective Witt asked, looking more interested than ever.

"Because my wife has been sleeping with her husband for the past eight months."

Raquel's breath got caught in her chest and she felt like she couldn't breathe. Alexander and Giselle knew each other before the trip? How could that be possible?

Raquel's voice was a shaky whisper, "They're having an affair?"

14

CRESCENDO

Noah saw the shock on Raquel's face as tears gathered in her eyes. She had been through so much, and if Giselle had anything to do with her accident, which Noah suspected, he would do any and everything possible to make sure she paid.

"Mr. Palmer, is it?" The lady detective asked.

"Yes, and you are?" Noah needed to get the names of both detectives. He had friends in high places, and nobody would stand in the way of Raquel getting justice. She was an innocent bystander in Giselle's mess, and she didn't deserve to suffer the consequences.

"I'm Detective Garner, and this is Detective Witt." She answered with a nod in the direction of her massive partner. Noah thought the man looked more like a professional wrestler than a detective.

"So you think your wife tried to kill Mrs. Vincent because of some illicit affair?" The large man asked, his dark eyes sparkling with interest.

"Yes. I know my wife. If she wanted Alexander and Raquel was in her way..." Noah didn't have to finish his statement for everyone to catch his meaning. Giselle would kill to get whatever she wanted.

The tears were freely flowing down Raquel's swollen face when Noah looked in her direction. He hated to see her cry, and it wasn't his intent to stress her out even more, so he asked if they could step outside to finish the questioning.

After stepping outside with the male detective, he continued to badger him with questions. Once they finished, Noah felt like he was a suspect. At least he could feel better knowing the detectives were doing their jobs and not just half-assing around.

Noah finished his unofficial interview and made his way back inside Raquel's room. The other detective was walking toward him when he entered. She gave him a small smile but didn't say anything as she exited the room.

"Are you okay?" Noah knew the simple question was stupid. But Raquel looked so defeated, and he just wanted to make her feel comforted.

"*No.*" She sniffled, wiping away tears. "But, I will be."

"I'm really sorry." Noah moved toward her and sat down in a chair next to the bed.

"For what? You weren't having the affair." Noah could hear the sadness in Raquel's voice.

"For breaking the news the way I did. You have enough to worry about without adding all of this on top," Noah explained, his voice laced with regret.

"At least now I know and I don't have to feel bad about asking him for a divorce," Raquel said, still wiping her tears away.

"According to the information I found, they'd been seeing each other for at least eight months. But I don't think they've been in contact since we've gotten back from Jamaica. Or at least not on a regular. I haven't confronted either Alexander or Giselle with what I've found out."

"Eight months?" Raquel shook her head. "I thought I imagined things. He told me I was insecure, and I needed to stop nagging him when I asked why he didn't pick up the phone and why he seemed to be working late more often. He even told me I was crazy when I smelled the perfume that wasn't mine in our home."

"You definitely weren't crazy. Giselle has been to your house several times." When Raquel raised an eyebrow in question, Noah explained.

"I have tracking devices on all our cars. Locations are recorded. She didn't know about the device."

"Oh, so you already didn't trust her then?" Raquel responded.

"No, it wasn't that. I know you don't know this, but I'm a private investigator. Mostly tech stuff nowadays, but in the past, I had my fair share of cheating spouse cases."

"I see. And it took you this long to figure out your wife was cheating?"

Noah couldn't help but chuckle. "I know it doesn't say much about my investigating skills, but I wasn't the most attentive husband. I was trying to change that and voilà, the cheating wife discovered."

"Well, shit."

"I know, right?" Noah sighed. "You're taking this better than I'd expected." He studied Raquel closely. Although she still had a sadness in her eyes, there was also a resolve that shown through.

Raquel shrugged then winced. "I keep forgetting about my clavicle. Anyway, I had already decided to move on with my life without Alexander. He recently shared that he didn't want kids *ever*. He lied to me for fifteen years, and I knew I wouldn't be able to forgive him. We've been separated for over a month. I sent the divorce papers this week."

"Wow. I'm sorry, Rocky. I know how much having kids means to you." Noah couldn't believe what a dumbass Alexander was to treat Raquel in such a horrible manner.

"Well, I got my wish anyway." Raquel rubbed her still flat belly with a smile and then she frowned. "I'm going to be a single parent." She sighed heavily.

Noah grabbed her hand tightly. "I'll be there for you and our baby. I promise."

"You can't promise something like that. You don't even know if the baby is yours yet." Raquel frowned.

"I know you don't know me yet, but I'm a man of my word, Rocky. I won't let you down." Noah was sincere, but he understood after everything Raquel had been through, he would have to earn her trust through actions and not words.

"We can schedule a noninvasive prenatal paternity test." Raquel's suggestion made sense, but it also made Noah nervous.

What if the baby wasn't his? What if their time had come to an end? What if he missed yet another chance to get to know Raquel?

Noah knew he probably shouldn't have been thinking about another woman, especially since he hadn't even confronted his wife about her cheating. But he knew his relationship with Giselle was over, and it had been for a long time.

The truth was, he and Giselle had grown apart, and instead of talking or even leaving, they decided to swing. At the time, it sounded fun and swinging *was* fun. Noah had greatly enjoyed it, but like he told Raquel, it didn't fix his marriage. Swinging shifted their focus.

Now it was time to think about the future. He might be a dad, but before he could concentrate on anything, he had to handle some business.

NOAH SPENT MOST OF THE DAY WITH RAQUEL, AND THEY MANAGED to get the paternity test scheduled for the following week. It was time for him to go back to Austin and face his wife.

Once he arrived home, the first thing he saw was Giselle's car in the driveway. Noah wasn't surprised she was home because he was sure Alexander had called to warn her. Giselle had been blowing his phone up since he'd had words with her "secret lover" the day before. Noah chose to ignore her. Instead, he'd spent his time helping Raquel cope with the idea of becoming parents. They spent most of the day talking about the intimate details about life and discussing how they would handle being parents.

When he walked into the house, Giselle was pacing back and forth while texting. It was like he was having a case of déjà vu. Noah hoped this time when he asked her questions she would tell him the truth.

"Noah! Thank God you're home. I didn't think you would come back!" Giselle exclaimed with shocked wide eyes.

"Why wouldn't I come home, Giselle?" Noah asked calmly as he sat down on the couch.

"I was visited by the police. What's going on?" Giselle ignored Noah's question and went straight into victim mode.

"Were you really at Penelope's the other night?" Noah could play the same game. He didn't have to answer shit. The time for playing coy was over and done with. Somebody has tried to kill Raquel and *his* baby. No, they didn't have the results in yet or even taken the test for that matter, but he was hopeful.

"What?" Giselle's nose wrinkled as if she smelled something sour, but her phony disposition was not fooling Noah. She knew exactly what he was asking her.

"You heard what I said. Were you at Penelope's?" Noah's cobalt eyes were cold as he glared at his future ex-wife.

"Of course, I was at Penelope's. God, Noah! What's with the third degree? You should have my back instead of telling the police I should be a suspect. What the hell is wrong with you?" Giselle's voice got louder and higher until she sounded like a squawking crow.

"If you haven't done anything, then why are you so upset? You *should* be a suspect! You have the motive to hurt Raquel because you've been fucking her husband for over eight months! What the fuck did you think?" Noah's nostril's flared, and his chest was heaving, but he remained seated, trying to control himself.

Giselle stumbled back as if he'd struck her. If Alexander had indeed called her, she shouldn't have been surprised by his words.

Noah didn't think Giselle's green eyes could get any wider, but she somehow managed. He would've laughed if their conversation weren't so serious. He wondered how he hadn't seen through Giselle's bullshit before, but then again, he wasn't concerned about what his wife was doing.

"How could you think so little of me? I wouldn't cheat on you or kill anybody." She looked away, tears filling her eyes.

Noah shook his head. His wife took him for an idiot. Hell, he was for a long time. What kind of investigator didn't know his wife was sleeping with another man behind his back for almost a year?

"Just because you think I slept with Alexander doesn't make it true." Giselle straightened her posture and held her head high. Noah could only nod. *Okay, so we're playin' this game.*

Technically, Giselle had a point. Noah had proof that Giselle was going to Dallas and her car was parked at Alexander's house for hours. He also had evidence that they'd only pretended not to know one another at the resort. However, he didn't have any solid proof they were having sex.

Anyone could assume, but pictures and the video were worth a thousand words. So Noah decided he wouldn't show Giselle his hand. She had no idea what evidence he had against her, and she was too arrogant not to run her mouth. All he had to do was wait and watch.

"It doesn't matter what I *think*, darlin', it's all in the evidence and you, my dear left plenty," Noah smirked.

Giselle's face crumpled, and Noah's smirk became a full grin. He had called her bluff, but she definitely wouldn't be calling his. Noah pulled his phone from his pocket and discreetly hit the voice record app. This conversation was going to get deep, and Noah needed to be smart.

"So what if you have *evidence?*" Giselle snarled as her face became red and her eyes glared evilly. "Alexander is more man than you'll ever be and he'll take care of me. I don't need you, Noah!" Giselle flung her arms wildly. Her usually neat hair was unkempt, and for the first time, Noah realized that his wife was becoming unhinged.

"The state of Texas will be taking care of you if you had anything to do with hurting Raquel," Noah growled, becoming more upset. Even though he knew of his wife's infidelity, it was still a tough pill to swallow to have it thrown in his face.

"Fuck you, Noah! I didn't have shit to do with hurting your precious, Raquel. I was at Penelope's, and there's *evidence* of that too, so go fuck yourself!" Giselle screamed at the top of her lungs before snatching up her phone and purse and storming from the room.

Noah paused the recording then immediately emailed it to himself. At least he wouldn't have to worry about her contesting the prenup when he filed for divorce. However, he was concerned about Giselle's insistence she had an alibi. Noah was sure she had something to do with Raquel's accident. He just had to prove it.

ALEXANDER

"If you admitted to Noah that we were having an affair, how does that help us, Giselle?" Alexander couldn't believe when Giselle had texted him to meet from her hotel room, in Dallas. She was supposed to be laying low until Raquel was out of the way.

"I admitted to what he already knew." Giselle waved her manicured hand dismissively.

Alexander hated when she treated him like an imbecile. It was his idea to take out the extra insurance policies on Raquel, and to get another woman to kill her. It was also his idea not to see each other after their trip to Jamaica, nobody was supposed to know that they'd been in a relationship.

"And that makes you look guilty, Giselle. They would've never had a reason to consider you a suspect. You gave them a fucking motive!"

"I wasn't the one who fucked this up, Alexander. I have an alibi. I was all the way in Austin when Raquel had her *accident*."

"I didn't fuck this up. I got us a patsy to take the fall, but Raquel just got lucky. The car flipped several times that should've done it." Alexander had made all the preparations to behave like a grieving spouse, and now he had to act like he gave a shit about his bitch of a wife.

"Well, I have a plan that will definitely finish that bitch off. But you have to stay away from the hospital, and get rid of your little girlfriend. That bitch is bat shit crazy."

Alexander narrowed his eyes. It seemed he had a tendency to attract insane women, Giselle included.

❧ 15 ❧

NOT ADDING UP

R aquel had been a sloppy mess since Detective Garner and Detective Witt's visit. As if the news of someone purposely cutting her brakes wasn't enough, Noah had to drop the bomb it could possibly be Giselle who had done it. As far as she knew, the detectives followed up on the lead, but she hadn't heard anything else thus far. Raquel felt it was off-putting to know someone was out there purposely trying to hurt her. She had no idea how her life had gotten so far out of control.

Alexander had stop trying to come to the hospital, but he wouldn't stop calling at least until Raquel had confronted him about his cheating, then he backed right off. However, he still refused to sign the divorce papers even though it was clear he didn't want to be in a relationship, at least with her. And now, she had to deal with a paternity test.

Raquel's nerves were shot, and she didn't know how much more she could take before she would have to be wrapped in a strait jacket and placed in a padded room.

Dr. Patton striding into her room, gained her attention. She needed to get out of the pity party she was throwing for herself anyway. The entire time Raquel had been in the hospital, it had been nothing but nonsense and foolishness surrounding her. She was sure she was the hottest topic on her floor and maybe of the entire hospital. Raquel hoped the doctor would have good news about her leaving soon.

"Hello, Mrs. Vincent. How are you feeling today?" Dr. Patton's brown eyes were kind as he studied her carefully, and Raquel felt a little of the tension leave her body.

"I'm still a little sore, but my head feels a lot better, and the nausea is almost completely gone," Raquel answered with a small smile.

Raquel wasn't at one-hundred percent yet. She was barely at forty, but she wanted to go home. Being in a hospital alone wasn't fun at all, at least in the comfort of her own home she could wallow in self-deprecation alone without fear of being gossiped about.

"The soreness will wear off eventually, but your body endured a traumatic experience. Healing is going to be a slow process, especially since we have to watch the types of medication we can give you." Dr. Patton began taking her vitals.

Raquel nodded, knowing what he'd said were facts, but again, she just wanted to leave.

"Everything looks okay except for your blood pressure. It's a bit higher than I would like it to be, so we'll keep an eye on it for now." The doctor checked her IV bag and commenced to scribbling something down on her chart.

"Did you have any questions for me?" Dr. Patton asked as he finished up all of the necessary checks.

"When do you think I'll be able to go home?" Raquel hadn't even been there an entire week, but nobody wanted to be in a hospital.

"Mrs. Vincent, I understand your anxiousness to go home, but I assure you we have your best interest in mind. We don't want to rush discharging you because you don't want to be here. Believe me, we will do everything possible and give you the best care, and we'll get you home as soon as we can." He patted her hand like a parent placating a child before turning and leaving the room without answering her question.

Raquel sighed, she knew the older man meant well and he was simply doing his job. However, it still didn't make her feel any better.

She looked out the window of her room, feeling the shadow of gloom hovering over her, but she wouldn't give in.

Her baby needed her to be healthy, so she had no other choice but to suck it up and get on with it. She needed to concentrate on getting better, but first, she would call in a favor to see just exactly what her husband had been up to.

If Alexander had been having an affair with Giselle for months and then dared to make sure they met, there was absolutely no telling what else or better yet who else he'd been doing. Raquel had already requested a full blood workup along with the paternity test. She'd hoped to goodness Alexander hadn't given her any STD's.

Raquel had started to doze off when the door creaking open woke her. She smiled when she saw who was sauntering in her room, holding a giant teddy bear and flowers.

"There's our girl. You scared the crap outta me." Patrice leaned down and gave Raquel a gentle squeeze as her husband Deaton stood quietly by waiting for his turn to greet Raquel. Once the hugs and kisses were given the couple settled into the chairs on the side of the bed.

Raquel had had plenty of visitors from colleagues to friends, but she was happy to see Patrice. She was the closest thing she had to family. Both of her parents had passed away, and she didn't have any siblings. Raquel had distant cousins somewhere in Oklahoma, but they didn't keep in touch.

"I scared you?" Raquel scoffed, "Believe me, you weren't the only one scared, honey." Raquel gave a weak smile, and Patrice gave her a sad smile in return.

"How're you feelin'?" Deaton's deep sultry southern twang would make any woman sit up and take notice, he reminded Raquel a lot of Noah, and it made her sad all over again.

"Tired, but fortunately, I'll live. Bumps, bruises and breaks won't keep me down." Raquel answered, trying to sound positive.

"Good. I'm glad to hear you still got some fight in ya." Deaton's voice turned concerned, and his gray eyes were full of curiosity, "So, Patrice said you needed a favor. What can I do for you, little lady?"

Deaton Elliot was a good friend to have in your corner. The high powered attorney made sure to put the fear of God into Alexander. However, Raquel's husband was bound and determined to keep the farce of a marriage together because he refused to sign the papers.

Deaton had promised Raquel he would put some of the best private investigators on her case. She would know within the week all of Alexander's misdeeds. Raquel wanted all the ammunition she could get, so when she claimed irreconcilable differences for the divorce, Alexander wouldn't be able to contest shit. She had enough to deal with concerning Alexander, but her job was also causing her major stress.

Raquel was on the phone to the counseling director, making sure all of her medical leave paperwork was completed and approved. It was great that she worked for a public school and had FMLA leave. Susan Waters, her director assured Raquel she had filled out everything correctly, and her, as well as human resources, approved her leave.

Raquel had to double-check with Ms. Waters because her principal had sent her a scathing email once again claiming Raquel didn't receive approval and could be written up or terminated. Although the wording seemed professional enough, Raquel got the underlying message.

That was the third time Ms. Strauss had threatened Raquel's job. And although they had had words at the beginning of the school year, Raquel didn't think it was reason enough for the woman to come after her job continually. There was something else going on, and it just wasn't adding up.

Raquel was finishing up her phone call when a soft knock sounded on the door.

"Come in," Raquel called out.

"Hey, darlin'." Noah's long legs were wrapped in a pair of jeans that fit his body to perfection. His blond hair flopped into his face covering up his sparkling blue eyes.

"Hey." Raquel sounded breathless, but she hoped Noah didn't catch the sound.

Raquel still felt the connection to Noah even though she didn't know him very well. It was all very ironic. Here they were preparing to be co-parents after spending a few wild weeks together, and their spouses had been together for months without either of them knowing.

"What are you doing back in Dallas?" Raquel asked, genuinely confused. Noah had given his DNA to be tested, and the results wouldn't be in for another five days. She hadn't expected to see him until then even though she was more than happy he was there.

Although it had ultimately been her choice, Raquel had basically been going through everything alone. She didn't want to deal with Alexander, and even though Patrice and Deaton had visited or at least called her every day, it wasn't the same.

"I came to check on my baby mama." Noah's face broke out in a Cheshire cat grin, and his eyes danced in amusement.

Raquel twisted her face in mock disgust, but it was so she wouldn't laugh at his silliness. "Anyway." She rolled her eyes as he came and took a seat beside her.

"How's the leg?" Raquel rubbed her hand over her cast at the mention of her leg.

"It hurts, but they give me a lot of good drugs." Raquel smiled to keep from crying. It would take months of rehab to be able to properly walk again. Add to that a growing baby bump and the future was looking a little shaky.

Noah nodded, and it looked as if he wanted to say something, but he was hesitating for some reason. Raquel wished she could just fast forward the time where they knew each other better, and they could talk to one another without fear. They had a long way to go. *Or not, he may not even be the father.*

"Have the police been back?" Noah finally asked. The tension in the room increased with his words. The police, in fact, had been back the day before.

Detective Garner walked into the room, and Raquel could instantly tell the woman carried a heavy burden. The thought scared her.

"Detective, did you find out any new information?" She was hopeful the

*downtrodden aura which surrounded the detective was because she was
exhausted from solving her case.*

*"Yes, actually we did find something new. Giselle Palmer was in an apart-
ment building in downtown Austin at the time of your car wreck. She was seen
on surveillance video." The detective answered solemnly.*

*Raquel wanted to cry at the news. If it wasn't Giselle who had cut her
brakes, then who in the hell did?*

*"Does your husband have any enemies? Anyone who would want to get to
him by hurting you?"*

*"I have no idea." Raquel rubbed her temple. She wished she could say
without a doubt that Alexander had nothing to do with her being hurt, but she
honestly didn't know.*

"We'll do everything in our power to solve your case, Mrs. Vincent."

The police didn't have any more solid leads, and Raquel wondered
if she should be worried. If someone was trying to kill her, there should
be some plausible explanation as to why. She didn't have enemies; she
was a public school counselor for goodness sakes.

Deaton should be calling her with information any day now.
Alexander was a senior financial analyst at Briscoe LLC. His job wasn't
exactly dangerous, but with the recent discovery of her husband's
duplicity, she didn't put anything past him.

"So, the police? Have they been back?" Noah asked again.

"Yes, the police came by and asked me if I had any enemies. I don't.
They think maybe this has to do with Alexander, but evidently, he told
the police he didn't have any enemies either." Raquel studied Noah
closely. It seemed like he knew something.

"Why do you ask? They cleared Giselle. Detective Garner said she
had an alibi." Raquel asked.

"Yeah, Giselle told me. She actually told me a lot of things." Noah
responded cryptically.

"Oh, really? Like what?" Raquel moved the bed so she could sit up
to see his face better.

"Giselle said she and Alexander had plans to be together. He's
going to divorce you so they can live happily ever after."

"Well, if that's the plan; why won't he sign the divorce papers. He keeps stalling, saying he wants to work it out especially if the baby is his." Raquel was beginning to get upset.

Raquel told Alexander she wouldn't even ask for child support if the baby was his. She made sure he understood signing over his parental rights was an option. Alexander could leave the marriage, and Raquel wouldn't ask for a thing. But he wouldn't sign.

"That's interesting. Maybe Giselle is delusional, and Alexander had no plans to ever divorce you. It wouldn't be the first time a married man told his mistress a lie about leaving his wife."

"Yeah, but something isn't adding up. Alexander admitted to me he didn't want children, I gave him an easy out, and he still wouldn't take it." Raquel was baffled by the entire situation.

"I may be able to help." Deaton's deep voice came from the door.

Raquel smiled in relief because she would finally know what was going on, but when she looked over at Noah, he had a deep scowl on his face. However, she would ask about his demeanor later, right now, it was time to get to the bottom of what was going on.

"Great! I knew you would come through for me, Deaton." Raquel smiled happily.

"I hate to wash that beautiful smile off your face, honey, but your husband has been extremely busy. For a long time."

Raquel's face dropped, "What do you mean by 'busy' and what's a long time?"

"I mean there have been multiple affairs, and I mean going back years. But that's not the worst part."

"Well, fuck." Raquel heard Noah grumble from the chair, but she couldn't focus on him right in that instant. As a matter of fact, she could feel herself getting nauseous.

"What's the worst part?" Raquel swallowed hard.

"Alexander has taken out multiple insurance policies on you."

"Alexander did this? He tried to kill me?"

❧ 16 ❧

REVELATIONS

Alexander was a slimy piece of shit who should be wiped off the planet. He was a poor excuse for a human being and a disgraceful husband. How could a person be so reprehensible? Noah would never understand someone like him. However, he now had a better understanding of why the relationship between Alexander and Giselle progressed so fast. They had similar ways of thinking. *Only about themselves.*

"In the past six years, Alexander has had around ten mistresses. He doesn't seem to discriminate, they are all shapes, sizes, color and creed. They do all have one thing in common though. They only last about two months at a time." Deaton revealed.

"Okay, so who are these women? What are the reasons for him cheating with them?" Raquel's voice was quiet.

"We didn't find out all the identities of the women, and I don't know his reasons were for cheating, sweetheart. That's something only that bastard knows. But as far as I can tell and from what the women we did find, they all said the same things. They were flings; nothing serious and some didn't even know he was married."

"I just don't understand why he would do this to me. Why would he try to kill me for insurance money now? We've been married for fifteen years. What is his motive?" Raquel's brows were drawn down and her face held in a frown.

"Unfortunately, my guys couldn't find a reason why he would do this. He didn't have any known enemies that we could find, and although he likes to gamble he didn't owe anyone any astronomical amounts of money. I'm sorry, Raquel, but he might just be greedy and was tired of working for a living." Deaton responded, his voice dripped with sadness.

AFTER LISTENING INTENTLY TO ALL OF THE INFORMATION DEATON Elliot revealed, Noah had an overwhelming need to protect Raquel. She was lying defenseless and hurt in a hospital bed, and her husband, of all people, had arranged the entire incident. Finding out about everything Alexander had done had Noah flabbergasted, and he decided right then and there he wouldn't leave Raquel's side.

As Deaton continued speaking, Noah had to admit he was thoroughly impressed with the other man's investigators. It was miraculous they were able to unearth such vital information. Alexander had kept so much hidden for many years. All of his foul deeds made Noah realize he should've been able to find out the same information.

However, not only was Noah unable to find out about Alexander's gambling addiction, he wasn't given any incriminating information against him at all. It was as if someone were blocking his access. But that couldn't be, because he had one of the best hackers in North Texas.

Noah decided from now on, he would look for the information himself instead of giving the assignment to someone else. Now that he knew what to look for, he could see if someone was actively blocking him.

"We need to call Detective Garner." Raquel's soft voice called for Noah's attention.

"I've already contacted the police, but I thought you should hear it straight from me what was going on. If I let the cops tell you, Patrice would've chapped my hide. Plus, I wanted to make sure you were gonna be alright." Deaton's deep voice held concern.

Noah could tell the man really cared for Raquel. It made him happy that she had good people in her corner, especially at a time like this. "What did the police say?" Noah asked. He knew some cops didn't take too kindly to civilians trying to "help" on cases.

"Garner said she would look into the information. But we both know that could take weeks if not months. I suggest you get a restraining order against Alexander as soon as possible, Raquel. You don't need to take any unnecessary chances."

"How am I supposed to do all that from a hospital bed, Deaton? It's not like I can petition the court from here. Dr. Patton said it would be another two weeks before I can even think about going home."

Noah could hear the frustration in Raquel's voice, and he felt terrible for her. He also felt helpless just sitting beside her bed watching her fret. So when the opportunity presented itself finally, he jumped at the chance to contribute.

"Don't you worry about goin' anywhere, darlin'. I have plenty of people who owe me favors. I'll take care of everything. *You* just focus on getting better."

Noah knew a few judges, but one in particular who would sign an order of protection for him on such short notice. So Raquel didn't have to worry herself. He would definitely take care of that for her. It was the least he could do.

"Noah, you really don't have to do that. This is not your responsibility at all. I'm just glad you're here. You don't have to get involved with this any more than you already are."

Raquel could say whatever she wanted, but convincing Noah after his mind was made up was impossible.

"Hey," he said softly, brushing her slightly bruised cheek. "I told you we were friends, and I'd always be here for you. I meant what I said. We'll handle this together. We'll handle *everything* together, okay?" Noah wanted to comfort Raquel, and he hoped she could hear the sincerity in his voice.

Noah needed her to know he was a man of his word. He would do anything and everything in his power to help her through such a difficult time, and after it was over, he hoped she would recognize that she could always count on him.

"Thank you for being here for me. I know this isn't the ideal situation." Raquel's smile was shaky, but Noah understood her pain.

"I wouldn't be anywhere else in the world but beside you, darlin'." Noah winked as he broke out his most charming smile. He could see the slight blush on Raquel's brown cheeks and the genuine smile on her face before she turned away.

"Well, I think I've overstayed my welcome." Deaton smirked as he moved toward the door. "You all have a good one. And if I find out anything else, I'll let ya'll know."

Once Deaton left, Raquel settled under the bed covers as her dark eyes zeroed in on Noah. The pain in the depths of her orbs was so imposing. It was like it had manifested itself and wrapped around his own heart. Words couldn't describe the connection he felt with this woman.

"I can't believe Alexander would do this to me. Even if he didn't want a family, why wouldn't he just let me go? I never thought he would stoop so low as to kill me for money. I spent years loving a man who would kill me for *money*."

"I'm sorry, Rocky. I know all of this is beyond hard and there's no advice I can give you to make you feel any better. Just know we'll make it through this. I'll be here every step of the way no matter what."

When the tears started to fall down Raquel's cheeks, leaving the evidence of despair and sadness in their wake, Noah couldn't contain the urge to kiss her. So he bent his head down until his firm lips met her succulent, plump ones. He kissed her like a dying man trying to steal her breath.

It had been so long since he had touched her in this way. God, help him, he enjoyed every minute of it. The feel of her lips, the taste of her tongue, and the sight of her heaving breasts were all too much for him to handle.

If they hadn't been in a hospital, Noah would've taken her right then and there. He wanted to make her feel something other than pain and sorrow. Noah wanted her to feel needed, unique, and loved. He wanted Raquel to feel special.

CIRCLE OF DECEIT

Noah slowly broke the kiss and pulled back to look into Raquel's beautiful face. She was vulnerable and he didn't want to take advantage of her. So as much as he hated to stop, he knew it was for the best.

"I'm going to get a nurse to bring a cot in here for me. Do you need anything?" Noah's voice was more intense than usual, and he cleared his throat to regain control.

"No, I'm okay," Raquel responded softly.

Noah noticed she didn't argue about him getting a cot to stay with her, so he counted it as a win.

⚜

LATER THAT NIGHT, NOAH DECIDED TO STEP OUT AND GET something to eat. Raquel had been given her medication and was completely knocked out, bless her heart. The news of Alexander's duplicity had taken a toll on her as well as the baby.

Noah couldn't wait to get his hands on him. That fuckin' little Napoleon asshole had some huge balls to treat a woman like Raquel the way he had. The little shit didn't deserve to breathe the same air as she did. His mistreatment of her was a tragedy.

As Noah stood in line waiting for his take-out order, his phone buzzed with a notification. He'd been impatiently waiting on word from his high-powered contacts since he'd connected with them earlier that evening. Noah called in every favor he had in order to get a protective order in place for Raquel. He couldn't take the chance on Alexander coming back and finishing the job while Raquel was vulnerable.

Noah looked at his phone. The words "It's done" appeared on the screen. It was one less thing he would have to worry about. Although it would only be temporary, Raquel's protective order was pushed through.

It was good to have friends in high places. Noah worked a case and caught a judge's wife having extracurricular activities with the pool boy, and in turn, it saved the man millions of dollars in the divorce.

Noah smiled to himself as he picked up his order and headed back to the hospital. He usually wouldn't have left Raquel, but before she

113

fell asleep, she was complaining about the hospital food and begging him to get food from the bistro around the corner.

After everything she had endured, Noah felt getting her the food she wanted was the least he could do. Catering to the mother of his child was something he didn't realize he wanted so badly. He never pictured himself as a father until he heard the doctor tell Raquel she was pregnant.

Something deep down inside told him he was the father of Raquel's baby. The hope that rose in his chest was undeniable, and Noah knew he would do everything in his power to provide for his child.

He knew it was beyond wishful thinking to have a relationship with Raquel, considering their current situation. But he couldn't help but think they were meant to be. Noah understood their cheating spouses had orchestrated their meeting. However, the two of them had a bond.

They shared more than sex. Their time together was intimate and cherished. And if they made a baby, it would solidify Noah's truth. He and Raquel had been thrown together by circumstance, but he hoped against hope they could stay together in love.

When Noah returned to Raquel's room, she was still sleeping. However, he noticed her head thrashing from side to side. Even in her sleep, she couldn't get peace. The anger that rushed through Noah at the thought was overwhelming.

He wasn't a very emotional man, but the last few weeks had taken its toll. The knowledge of his wife's betrayal, the subsequent backlash Raquel was facing from her husband, and the uprooting of life as he knew it was astronomical. He felt anger, hurt, and dismayed. Noah just wanted to be happy.

Raquel moaned loudly as if she were in pain, and Noah rushed immediately to her side. He began to shake her gently to try and wake her up, but her eyes wouldn't open.

"Raquel, sweetheart? Wake up. Please wake up!" Noah shook her a little harder but to no avail. Raquel wasn't moving, and her breathing became labored.

"Darlin', it's Noah. Open those pretty eyes for me. Come on, baby, wake up!" When the heart monitor started going crazy, Noah began to panic. "Shit! What the hell is happening?"

Something was terribly wrong, but before panic could completely set in, a set of doctors and nurses began to rush into the room.

"Please step aside, sir!" someone yelled at Noah.

He had clearly heard the command, but couldn't get his feet to move. He hovered helplessly over Raquel, knowing he was in the way, but Noah wanted to help her. He *needed* to.

Scattered questions quickly ran through his brain. *How could this have happened? What had actually happened? How the hell could I have let this happen? She was fine before I'd left.*

Although still in a daze, Noah was finally able to leave Raquel's side when a nurse's firm hand landed on his shoulder. He stood silently in the room watching as the team frantically raced to save Raquel's life.

Noah's dull eyes were unfocused as they transferred Raquel to a gurney and rushed her out of the room. He couldn't believe one person could have so much misfortune. It was not a coincidence that something had happened after his departure from Raquel's hospital room. Someone had done this, and if it took until the last breath in his body, Noah was going to find out who and make them pay with their *life*!

⚜ 17 ⚜

FEVER PITCH

ALEXANDER

"Shit! She keeps fucking calling me!" Alexander shouted as he scrubbed a rough hand down his face. He was held up in a hotel in a small town outside of Dallas. Giselle had a friend who hacked the system and erased all of his known whereabouts. He was hiding because he was a suspect in the attempted murder of his wife, and he had to lay low until he could get the insurance money after she was pronounced dead. He also had to be far away from the hospital when Raquel met her maker. He had no idea how he'd gotten to this sad point in his life.

That was a lie, he knew exactly how he ended up in this shit show of a life. He trusted, Giselle. He blindly went along with her plans like her pussy was made of gold. He had a good life. He'd have his affairs ever so often to curve his itch for other women, and Raquel was never the wiser. He'd been doing what he wanted for fifteen years until that faithful day he lost all of his mind over one woman.

"I told you to cut that crazy bitch loose. She's no good to us now. Raquel should finally be dead. We can move on with our lives millions of dollars richer." Giselle's eyes were blissfully evil, and the sight made Alexander shudder.

"I can't just 'cut her loose' she knows too much. We have to get rid of her somehow." Alexander began to pace as he tried to think of a way to get rid of the nuisance of a woman.

"We? Are you speaking French? Because I already made arrangements for your dearly departed wife, now you want me to kill your girlfriend too. Damn, what good are you?" Giselle's condescending tone made Alexander want to strangle her ass.

"I can't be connected with the disappearance of anyone especially when they're trying to connect me to Raquel's accident."

"The cops are looking at you because they always have to investigate the spouse. If you get rid of your girlfriend, then they won't have a connection. Get. Rid. Of. Her." Giselle's tone was demanding, but Alexander knew she was right. It was time to clean up his mess.

☙❧

RAQUEL WAS IN CRITICAL CONDITION, AND NOAH'S RACING heartbeat was nowhere near slowing down. He feverishly paced back and forth in front of the ICU ward she'd been placed in. Legally, the doctors wouldn't give him any information because her slime-ball husband was still listed as her next of kin. However, Noah was able to get the protective order paperwork rushed to the hospital to keep Alexander from being able to make any medical decisions on Raquel's behalf.

The only other person listed to receive information for Raquel's condition was her best friend, Patrice, and as soon as Noah called Deaton to let them know what had happened, the couple rushed to the hospital.

So, while Noah wore a path in the shiny, white tile of the hospital's floor, Patrice talked privately with Raquel's doctors about her condition.

"Hey, man your footprints are gonna be permanently embedded in the damn floor. You need to sit your ass down 'cause you're makin' me nervous." Deaton's country twang stopped Noah in his tracks, but there was no stopping the continuous loop of dread that filled his chest.

Noah exhaled a deep breath and reluctantly sat down beside Deaton. His strong hands swiped through his disheveled hair for the millionth time. His face was covered in dark stubble, and he desperately needed a shower. However, his first priorities were Raquel and the baby. The last time he left her alone, she'd ended up in critical condition.

"What do you think really happened? 'Cause I know a fractured leg doesn't equate to a code blue." Deaton said the words that Noah had yet to express out loud.

Whatever had happened to Raquel while Noah was gone was no accident. Someone had deliberately done something, which meant someone in the hospital had to know something.

"Foul play," Noah responded simply.

"Alexander?" Deaton's brows were furrowed as his eyes narrowed in suspicion.

"I haven't been able to check the surveillance feed from the hospital entrances yet, but I don't think he would've gotten in so easily after Raquel removed him from the visitation list."

"Well, I assume you need some high-speed tech since you're not leaving, right?" Deaton questioned.

"I'm definitely not going anywhere, and I'd appreciate any help you can give me."

Deaton nodded his head. "Say no more. You'll have everything you need within the hour. Raquel is family to Patrice and me, and we'll get that son of a bitch if it's the last thing I do."

"Thanks. This shit is messed up and being here without all my equipment is fucking with my head. Sitting and not doing anything is driving me crazy." Noah admitted.

He was done being the hopeless sidelined bystander. His mistakes had triggered this chaos, and he refused to let it go on any longer.

After Deaton left, Noah sat alone as he continued to wait on Patrice. It had been at least an hour since she'd been taken back for a private conversation with the doctor, and the little patience he had left was waning. So Noah decided to contact the detectives one more time.

"Hello, I need to speak to Detective Witt." They needed to be aware that Raquel was in imminent danger. They could no longer afford to play the waiting game. Alexander needed to be off the streets as soon as possible.

"Dallas Metro Police Department. Where may I connect your call?" The pleasant voice asked.

"Detective Witt please."

Noah only had to wait a few minutes, but it felt like an eternity before his call was answered.

"Detective Witt, speaking."

"Detective. It's Noah Palmer. There was an incident with Raquel Vincent last night."

※

RAQUEL COULD'VE SWORN IN HER HAZINESS THAT SHE HEARD Patrice's voice along with Noah's. But she couldn't be sure what they were talking about. She couldn't seem to open her eyes, and her mouth felt like she'd been eating cotton.

She took inventory of the rest of her body. She could feel all of her limbs, and even though they felt heavy, she could move them. Her hearing seemed to work just fine, and if she could manage to pry her eyes open, maybe she could tell if she could see.

"She's moving. Oh, my goodness! Raquel, can you hear me?" Raquel could hear the distress in Patrice's high-pitched voice. Since her throat felt like the Mojave Desert, she didn't try to speak. She simply nodded her head.

"Thank God!" Raquel would recognize that deep Texas drawl anywhere. Noah was there.

"I'll get the doctor," Patrice said.

"Darlin', can you talk?"

Raquel shook her head as she struggled to lift her hand to her throat. Hopefully, Noah would understand the signal for water. When she heard movement in the room and then felt a straw to her lips, she knew he'd gotten her unspoken message. Raquel tried not to gulp the water, but the feeling was so heavenly that she couldn't help herself.

"Slow down, darlin'. You're gonna choke."

Raquel wanted to scream when she felt the straw leave her lips. "W —what... what happened?" The croak in her voice was unrecognizable. She wondered how long she'd been out. The last thing she remembered was feeling hungry and never getting a chance to eat.

"You were poisoned, honey." The gloom Raquel heard in Noah's voice made her heart ache even more. She had no idea what she'd done to deserve all of the bad things that were happening to her.

"H-how? Who d-did... did this?" Raquel couldn't hide the shakiness in her voice, but the warmth from Noah's large hand covering hers gave her a sense of comfort.

"We don't know who did it yet. But it looks like someone slipped the poison in with your medication either through your pills or IV. So everyone who has been in your room is being questioned."

"The baby?" Raquel was afraid to hear the answer to that question because there was only one heart monitor. Although there wasn't a fetal heart monitor before, after being poisoned, Raquel could only assume they would want to monitor the baby.

When Noah didn't answer right away, Raquel was able to find the motivation to pry her eyes open. Her dark eyes instantly connected with the dull blue of Noah's piercing gaze. Raquel knew. Tears rolled down her cheeks before she could stop them. Her baby was gone. An innocent soul had been lost forever behind nonsense and foolishness.

"I'm sorry, darlin'." Noah's strong arms wrapped around Raquel's shaking body in comfort. But all she could feel was numbness.

"But, w-why?" Raquel hiccupped out a wailing sob. Her body racked with tension and sorrow.

"Shhh. It'll be okay. I'll make it okay."

Noah's softened voice helped Raquel release her tears without shame. She cried out her anger, frustration, and hurt. The unconditional love she felt for the baby she no longer carried now seemed to be a heavy burden. The hole in her heart from the loss was beyond devastating. The beautiful angel who she would never meet would always be a part of her broken heart.

"I just don't understand why." Raquel couldn't calm down. Her life was in shambles, and it was her fault.

She had made so many mistakes, and instead of correcting her wrongs, she'd continued to ignore them. Raquel would've never been in this situation if she'd stood up to Alexander in the first place.

It was okay to compromise in a relationship but not to the detriment of your self-worth. Raquel learned her lesson the hard way, and it was time she faced her faults head-on.

"I want to contact the police. They need to press charges against that son of a bitch. He won't get away with killing my baby." Raquel could hear the conviction in her voice. She would no longer be the weak push-over everyone saw her as.

Alexander would pay for what he did to her. He wouldn't get away with it, and if it were the last thing she did, Raquel would make sure her soon to be ex-husband paid. Even if it was with his life. *An eye for an eye...*

※

RAQUEL NOW HAD TWENTY-FOUR-HOUR SURVEILLANCE. THE POLICE department had received a little nudge from the mayor after Noah made a few phone calls. It was amazing how many people owed him favors.

In the following weeks, Raquel and Noah spent almost every waking hour together. And because she was still laid up in bed with a healing leg, there wasn't much for them to do besides talk.

Raquel asked Noah why he continued to stay since there was no longer anything tying them together, and he replied, "A bond like ours never goes away." Those words said so confidently by a man who stood by her at the most horrible time in her life, meant more than Raquel could ever say. So when the tests results came back, Raquel and Noah both agreed to have them destroyed. She didn't want to know if Alexander was the father of her lost baby. To think about him killing his own child was too much for her to bear.

However, Noah was there, standing by her side and being the rock Raquel hadn't known she'd needed. When she's first found out about Alexander's infidelity, she was prepared to raise the baby on her own. She had never expected Noah to show up and want to be a part of the baby's life, and without even knowing paternity, he was there supporting her.

"I'm so ready to get out of this place." Raquel moaned her displeasure of being cooped up in the room for nearly six weeks. Her leg was almost healed from the fracture, and if it hadn't been for the poisoning, she would be home.

"Doc Patton said you can go home tomorrow." Noah responded from "his" chair as he flipped through the channels on the TV.

"Yeah, I know. But I could've been gone by now if..." Raquel's voice became small as she trailed off. The thought of losing her baby made her throat tighten and her eyes instantly water.

"Well, darlin', you'll be on your way tomorrow, so stop worrying." Noah pulled her hand to his lips and kissed her knuckles.

He was always showing her affection in many ways—a kiss on her forehead, temple, and even small brushes of his lips against hers sweetly. But he never deepened the kiss or touched her inappropriately.

The care and consideration he showed her was more than she'd ever experienced in her life, and it made her regret some of her life choices. But life wasn't about regretting. It was about lessons, and she definitely learned hers.

"So, when are you going back to Austin?" Raquel anxiously blurted out the question because otherwise, the words would've been forever stuck rattling around her brain.

The last thing she wanted was for Noah to leave, but logically, she knew he wouldn't be in Dallas forever. His life was back in Austin, and she was a grown woman who should be able to stand on her own.

"Are you tryin' to get rid of me, Rocky?" He asked with a smirk covering his gorgeous face. Raquel stared into his curious gaze, searching for the words to express how she felt. But she didn't want to be a burden. The last thing she wanted was to come across as a needy, whiny woman. Hell, she *was* needy, but she didn't want Noah to see her that way.

"No." Raquel took a deep breath, garnering up the courage to finish her thoughts. "I know you have to go home eventually. I just want to be prepared for your departure."

"Departure? Why are you soundin' so formal? What's really on your mind, Rocky? And don't give me this politically correct bullshit or what you think I want to hear." She could hear the sternness in Noah's voice.

"I'm afraid... to be alone." Raquel's head was bowed in shame. She had never seen herself as weak before, and it was a hard pill to swallow to admit she needed help.

Raquel felt a dip in the bed as Noah sat beside her. He lifted her head and looked her in her eyes. "As long as I'm breathin', you'll never have to be alone again."

The emotions once again overwhelmed Raquel, and before she knew it, the tears were flowing. She was sick and tired of crying and feeling sorry for herself. She wished she could skip straight to the part where she was healed. And in all honesty, Raquel was scared that she would never be whole again.

"Noah, it's been a lot of emotions mixed up in this situation. I think we're clinging to each other because we've both been hurt. I just don't want to have to depend on you, and then poof, you're gone."

"I will not..." A knock on the door interrupted Noah's words.

"Mrs. Vincent. There was a call. Your husband has been reported missing," the uniformed officer barged in without any consideration.

"Missing? Who reported him missing?" Raquel sure as hell hadn't filed any reports, and with the restraining order against him, Alexander wasn't exactly making his presence known around the hospital.

"Uh. It says here..." The officer grabbed a small pad out of his pocket and flipped a few pages. "Oh, here it is. Ms. Jana Strauss."

"What? Why would my principal file a missing person's report for my husband? What the hell is happening right now?" Raquel asked.

"Yeah. It says here she's his girlfriend." The officer delivered the devastating news like he was giving a weather report. Raquel had no idea who the man was and why he'd been sent to tell her about the report. There were already detectives working her case and not that it would have made the news any easier to hear, but Raquel would've liked to have thought that Detective Garner would've had a little more tact when telling her about yet another woman her husband was sleeping with.

"*Girlfriend?* What the fuck?" Noah's voice was full of anger, and that's exactly what Raquel was thinking.

What the fuck?

❧ 18 ❧

KILLER AFFAIRS

ALEXANDER
"I have to go back to the house while I can. There's important documents and cash in the safe." Alexander tried to explain to Giselle but she was too wrapped up in her "plan" to comprehend what he was telling her.

"This is a mistake. You should be laying low. We can't be seen together." Giselle argued.

"Fine, you can stay in the car or drop me off. Whatever. But I'm going to get that money." Alexander stated with finality.

He never would've guessed that Giselle was right about it being a mistake to go home. He stood with his hands up as he tried to convince the woman that everything he'd said was the truth, and he loved her with all of his heart.

"You don't love me. You tried to play me for a fool, but not anymore Alexander. We had a plan, and you betrayed me!"

"That's not true. I did all of this for you. I want to be with you..."

Alexander didn't get to finish his sentence because the gunshot was unexpected. And the last thing he thought was what a huge mistake he'd made by taking Raquel for granted.

NOAH

The depth of Alexander's betrayals knew no bounds. After Noah cussed out the officer and kicked his rude ass out of Raquel's room, he contacted Detective Witt immediately.

"Why the fuck would ya'll send some no-named ass uniform here to tell Raquel about her piece of shit ex?"

"Palmer? What the hell are you talking about?" Witt questioned gruffly. Noah could tell by the man's tone of voice he wasn't being facetious, so he proceeded to explain what had happened.

"First of all, I would never send some nitwit to handle such sensitive information. I know you may not believe it or trust what I'm saying, but I will check into who gave the officer the authority to deliver the news to Mrs. Vincent. I apologize."

Noah believed him, but he was still pissed as hell. Raquel couldn't seem to catch a break from being hurt. "Whatever. But I know one thing. That shit better not happen again, or ya'll are going to have a big fuckin' problem. And believe me, this ain't the problem you want." That would be the only warning Noah gave. He'd meant every word out of his mouth. Raquel wouldn't continue to suffer if he could help it.

"Listen, the guy may have been completely out of line..."

"May have been?" The incredulous tone rose in Noah's voice as he cut off the detective's explanation.

"But what he said was true." Witt continued as if Noah hadn't uttered a word. "Alexander is missing, and Raquel's employer is the one who filed the report. According to Ms. Strauss, she and Alexander had been seeing each other for over a year. It wasn't something she was willing to admit at first, but we refused to take her statement unless a prior relationship was established."

Every time Noah didn't think he could be shocked anymore, he would learn more about Alexander Vincent and be proven wrong. The man was not only sleeping with Giselle and promising her the world; he was having an affair with Raquel's boss.

Although Deaton found evidence of multiple affairs, Jana Strauss' name had never come up. Alexander had obviously buried that secret deep.

But now, everything Raquel had told him about her job made so much more sense. The way the other woman was constantly berating Raquel or trying to find reasons to write her up and reprimand her. The woman had been acting out of jealousy the entire time.

Noah briefly wondered if Giselle knew about her so-called "lover." The last time Noah had seen her, she claimed to be leaving to start her life with Alexander. Noah didn't stop her or even care what she did anymore. When he found out about her cheating, he was done.

The only time Noah put in any effort to find Giselle was to serve her with divorce papers. He'd had them drawn up, signed, and sent to her the first two weeks he was in Dallas. And although he hadn't heard from her yet, Noah knew she'd received the papers because she'd signed for them.

Now, Noah thought that maybe he should look into where his future ex-wife actually was. He knew from the daily check-ins from his small office team that Giselle hadn't been by the business. Noah also knew that she hadn't been back to their house since she'd stormed angrily away. He'd been smart enough to get the locks and alarm code changed, and there hadn't been any disturbances reported.

"Palmer? Mr. Palmer? Are you still there?" Noah had completely blanked out on his conversation with the detective. He had so much shit to figure out and he was sure talking to the police wouldn't do him any good.

"Yeah, yeah, I'm here." Noah finally answered.

"Good. Like I was saying, I'll look into who sent the officer so it won't happen again." Witt answered, but Noah didn't care what the detective said. He didn't care if he had to play bodyguard and screen every person beforehand. He would make sure nobody got close enough to pull the same shit again.

"Uh, huh. Do ya'll suspect something bad happened to the asshole? Or did he, as a grown man, decide to up and leave one of his mistresses?" The contempt was dripping from every word Noah uttered. He couldn't wait for the day he got to kick Alexander's ass.

"Honestly. No idea yet. According to the woman, he's been missing a week. We checked his job, and they haven't seen him either. However, they didn't report him missing because he said he would be working from home. But there was no sign he'd been at home either."

"Strange." Noah wouldn't tell the detective about him hacking into the hospital camera's and not seeing Alexander. Noah was convinced the man had something to do with Raquel's poisoning, but the coward wasn't the one who'd given it to her.

Noah would check the feed for the fourth time to make sure he hadn't missed anything. He would also get Deaton to run a few checks to cover all the bases.

"Yeah, really strange. Anyway, I don't think Mrs. Vincent should go home when she's released. Her protection ends when she gets out of the hospital."

"I understand. And she won't be alone. Thanks for the info, Detective. I'll be in touch."

Noah disconnected the call and went to get his borrowed computer. Raquel was in her last therapy session with the guard, so he had the room to himself. As Noah waited for the computer to boot up, he gave Deaton a call.

The man was eager to help in any way he could, so Noah was sure he would have some clue as to where Alexander had gone before the night was over.

Once the computer finished loading, Noah logged into his program and started reviewing the surveillance videos again. Then he finally caught a break.

He picked up the computer and enlarged the screen. "I'll be a monkey's uncle."

Noah had no idea how he'd missed it before. He was so focused on seeing Alexander; he missed the woman with the platinum blond hair dressed in the nurse's uniform. It was the same woman he'd seen with Giselle.

"Shit! Giselle is involved in this up to her elbows!"

"I STILL DON'T UNDERSTAND WHY I CAN'T GO TO MY *OWN* HOME,

Noah. I've been in the hospital for six weeks and I want to lie down in my own bed."

Raquel's pleading voice almost broke his resolve, but Noah stood firm. He wouldn't take another chance with Raquel's safety by going to a house that Alexander had access to.

"Listen, darlin', I understand you want to go home, but it's not safe there. We'll stay in a nice fancy hotel for a few days until I can guarantee the house is secure." Noah answered, pulling an exhausted Raquel into his arms.

"I'm not trying to be difficult. It's just so many things have changed, and I want to feel something familiar. You know?"

Raquel's eyes were cloudy with pain, and Noah had the sudden urge to kiss her soft lips. So he did.

Raquel moaned into his mouth and pushed her body close to his. Noah pulled her closer, being mindful of her new walking boot cast. He slipped his hands down to her round ass and squeezed.

Noah had every intention of letting things go slow and not taking advantage of Raquel's vulnerability. But he could no longer hold himself back. It was simple. He wanted her. Over the past two months getting to know Raquel and watching how she was so strong and determined, made him fall deeply in love.

When Raquel loudly moaned again, Noah broke the kiss. With his forehead pressed against hers, they stood breathing in each other. The silence of the room crackling with sexual tension made Noah want to strip her clothes off and devour her body.

However, as much as he wanted to ravish her very being, he wouldn't. Both of them had a lot of healing and growing to do, but that didn't mean he wouldn't steal a kiss from time to time. Noah just had to remember to stay in control. Raquel was hurting, and he would comfort her, but he wouldn't take advantage.

"Why'd you stop?" Raquel's sweet voice whispered, breaking the quiet moment.

"You're not ready, Rocky." Noah was being honest, and Raquel's heavy sigh let him know she knew he was speaking the truth.

"Let's get you to this hotel, so we can have a nice rest and get some dinner." Noah kissed the top of Raquel's head.

They left the hospital after a flurry of goodbyes and well wishes from the hospital staff. It was amazing how many faces Noah recognized. After reviewing the surveillance video from the hospital several times, he made sure he memorized faces and names of everyone who had to come into contact with Raquel. It was something he should've done before to prevent her poisoning. However, because he dropped the ball, Noah was determined to get it right this time.

Although logically, he knew Raquel's poisoning wasn't his fault, he took the blame for leaving her alone. Noah had done so many things wrong with Giselle, and one thing he regretted the most was not showing her how much he loved and cared for her.

Noah once worshipped the ground Giselle walked on, and without realizing it, he stopped showing her his love. He began just to give her what she wanted, thinking that would make her happy. He thought money would fix everything, so every time she was upset, he bought her a gift or took her on vacation.

Noah's neglectful ways had contributed to Giselle's feelings of inadequacy. And although he wanted to take the blame for her cheating, he wouldn't because her infidelity was *her* choice. She could've chosen to talk to him and work on their relationship, but instead, she chose another man, and Noah couldn't forgive her.

Out of all the things they had done in their relationship, he never worried about infidelity. Noah thought because Giselle wanted to swing, she would get the need for other men's attention out of her system. Noah wasn't really bothered by the fact Giselle needed the recognition from other men. He'd known her for a long time, and he'd accepted who she was.

As long as they communicated about their sexual desires and needs, he was accepting of their extra-marital sexual conquests. However, when she began being deceitful, Noah had to draw the line.

"So you know we're going to have to go to my house if you insist on staying at a hotel, right?" Raquel looked up at him from the wheelchair.

Even though Raquel had a walking boot, it was hospital policy that patients leave in a wheelchair, and she was not happy about it.

"We can go to your house for some of your things." When Raquel smiled brightly, Noah chuckled and shook his head. He didn't want to give her anymore grief. So he easily agreed.

Once they got to Noah's vehicle, he helped her into the passenger's seat, and they were on their way. For some odd reason, Noah felt anxious about going to Raquel's home. The first time he had gone there was when he found out about her accident, and he never wanted to feel that type of panic again.

Noah also didn't like that he was unable to do a security check on the house before he took Raquel. He hoped Alexander wasn't lurking around or Giselle for that matter.

It was around six in the evening when they pulled up to Raquel's home. The sun was still shining, and people were milling around, so some of the anxiousness Noah felt faded.

"Okay, just get a few necessities. We can buy whatever else you need later. Then once I do a thorough check, we can come back and get more of your things."

"I'm not going to live in a hotel forever, Noah. Although I'm on leave from my job right now, at some point, I'm going to have to get back to my life." Raquel answered with exasperation coloring her words.

Noah understood her frustrations. She had already expressed how displaced she felt with her life being turned upside down. However, Raquel could not just go back to living life as usual when someone was trying to kill her.

"Rocky, darlin', I understand you want to go back to normal. But someone tried to kill you not once but *twice*. You have to move with caution until Alexander is caught." Noah hated to be so blunt, but he couldn't let Raquel think just because she was out of the hospital that everything was in the clear.

Tears came to Raquel's eyes, but before they fell, she sniffed hard and straightened her shoulders. "You're right. Let's get this over with so we can get out of here."

"That's my girl." Noah leaned over and kissed her softly on the lips. He hopped out and went around and opened Raquel's door.

Before she could shuffle too far ahead of him, Noah stopped her. "Hold up. Let me get my gun out of the car. Better safe than sorry."

Raquel frowned, but she didn't comment as Noah tucked his Glock into his waistband. They made their way to the front door when Noah spotted Mrs. Pitman at the front window of her house. He nodded in acknowledgment, and the older woman gave a nod and smirk in response. Noah found the woman odd, but he didn't think much of it.

"Hand me the keys, and I'll go in first," Noah stated as he turned his attention back to Raquel.

"Uh, Noah, the door is open." Raquel whispered with wide eyes.

Noah looked at the cracked door and instantly pulled out his gun. "Stay here. Better yet, go to Mrs. Pitman's house and call the police."

"We *both* should go to Mrs. Pitman's. I don't want you to go in there by yourself, Noah. *Please.*" Raquel pleaded.

Despite Raquel's concern, Noah couldn't let a threat go. There was no telling how long the police would take getting to them.

"The cops take too long sometimes. You could be in danger now. Go! I need you to call the police and Deaton. I'll check it out and be there soon. I promise!" Noah kissed her lips again and gently turned her around and nudged her toward the neighbor's house.

When Raquel disappeared inside, Noah cautiously opened the door wider and stepped in. He instantly knew to always trust his instincts that something was wrong because lying on the floor covered in blood was none other than Alexander.

❦ 19 ❦

TORMENT

Raquel knocked on Mrs. Pitman's door, and without preamble, it swung open. Frown lines creased the older woman's face, and the corners of her usually bright wide eyes were turned down with worried.

"Hi, Mrs. Pitman. Can I come in please?" Raquel asked.

The older woman's expression threw her off because Mrs. Pitman was always smiling and telling other people's business. It was unlike the older woman to look so distressed. "Oh, yes, of course. Come on in, honey. Are you doing okay? You've been in the hospital for quite some time. Your stay was much longer than anybody expected." Mrs. Pitman shot off a thousand questions as she led Raquel into her spacious sitting room and offered her a seat.

"I'm doing better. I just stopped by to pick up some things before heading out. I just need to make a quick phone call if you don't mind."

Mrs. Pitman nodded and excused herself to the kitchen. Raquel tried to make her comment as vague as possible because she knew Mrs. Pitman would be discussing this visit later with anybody who would listen.

When Mrs. Pitman left, Raquel called Detective Garner and relayed the details of how she found her door open, and Noah was inside. The detective immediately went on alert and told Raquel that she and her partner as well as a squad car were on the way. Even though the police were coming, Raquel still couldn't relax because Noah was in the house without any help. So she quickly called Deaton and told him what was going on.

Deaton was in his car and on the way before they disconnected the call. Because they lived so close, Raquel was sure he would be there in less than fifteen minutes, so she calmed slightly. Once she finished her calls, Mrs. Pitman sauntered into the living room with cups of tea. It was fitting for a woman who was always telling other people's business. Raquel smiled at the irony, but she accepted the drink without comment.

"Thank you. I wanted to wait for the police because my door was open just now. Have you seen anyone around my house?" Raquel asked, knowing the woman had.

"Hmm. Well, I saw your *husband* there earlier with some woman. You know you could do much better than a bottom feeder like him." Mrs. Pitman tsked with disgust.

Raquel didn't want to reveal to the gossiping woman that her marriage was done, divorce was on the horizon, and Alexander tried to kill her. But she did want to know why the police thought Alexander was missing if he was at her house. She also wanted to know what woman had been in her home.

"What time was he there?" Raquel asked as she moved toward the door. She needed to warn Noah so he wouldn't be caught off guard.

"Oh, I'd say about an hour or two ago. I saw one woman leave but not Alexander." Mrs. Pitman's face was still held in a frown.

"What did the woman look like?" Raquel asked as she texted Deaton and Detective Garner.

"Well, the first one was a skinny white woman with blond hair." Mrs. Pitman responded, but when she kept talking, Raquel stopped moving toward the door. "But the other woman was a little chunky thing with brown hair." Mrs. Pitman sucked her teeth again.

"Wait! Are you saying there were *two* women in my house?" Raquel responded, trying to hold in her anger.

"Yes, honey." Mrs. Pitman patted the back of Raquel's hand in sympathy. "I told you that husband of yours was a bottom feeder. Having all those floozies in and out of your house while you're in the hospital." She tsked again. "Just shameful."

"Hold on. So both women were there at the same time?" Raquel asked, confused.

"No. The chunky one was there after the blond left. But the blond one and Alexander arrived together." Mrs. Pitman's words were sure.

"Thanks, Mrs. Pitman." Raquel flung over her shoulder as she left her neighbor's house. She'd never been so glad to have such a nosy neighbor before, but she was honestly thankful for Mrs. Pitman.

As soon as Raquel stepped onto Mrs. Pitman's porch, she saw Deaton's big, red pick-up pull up into the circular driveway. Raquel knew Deaton had to be flying to make it to her house in such a short amount of time. She limped as fast as she could to the truck with her boot slowing her down.

"Deaton, thank you for coming so fast." Raquel gave him a big appreciative hug when he met her in front of his vehicle.

"Of course. Now, you owe me 'cause your best friend is pissed that I left her at home, so you need to call and calm her little ass down." Deaton responded with a smile.

Raquel chuckled. "I will definitely call her."

Before they could finish their conversation, Noah came barreling out of the front door. Raquel could tell by the urgency in his steps, something was wrong.

"Did you call the police?" Noah's voice was rushed, his face was flushed, and his hair was in disarray.

"Yes, and they're on their way. What's going on?" Raquel asked, her nerves on edge.

Noah shook his head, but the look he gave to Deaton was one she couldn't decipher. Raquel looked back in forth between the two men as they seemed to be communicating silently. She didn't know they knew each other well enough to have a secret eye language.

"What? Why are you two looking at each other like that? Just tell me what the hell is happening!" Raquel's loud voice was full of frustration.

"Alexander is inside," Noah replied.

Raquel's anger was palpable as she began limping toward her front door. However, before she could pass Noah, he wrapped her around the waist and stopped her from moving forward.

"No, darlin'." Those two words held so much emotion. Raquel knew deep down in her soul why Noah didn't want her to go into the house, but she didn't want to accept it.

"Alexander is dead."

֎֍֍

RAQUEL SAT IN A DAZE AS SHE ANSWERED THE DETECTIVE'S questions. It was amazing how quickly hate could turn to sorrow in a blink of an eye. Before leaving the hospital, Raquel could honestly say she hated her husband. He betrayed her in ways she would have never expected. He had broken her heart and stolen her time. Raquel was ready to never see him again in life.

Now, Alexander was gone *forever.* He was never coming back, and Raquel was filled with regret. The disappointment she felt because of the crumble of her relationship was overwhelming.

She had never known that one person could experience so much loss so quickly. The loss of her relationship, the loss of her baby, and the loss of Alexander were very tragic. It was all too much. However, the tears wouldn't come. For the first time in what felt like forever, Raquel felt numb. The only thing Raquel could think to do was pray. She prayed for patience, health, knowledge, and understanding. And with all her might, she prayed for strength.

"I think that will be enough questions for today. If you need anything else from Raquel, you can give me a call."

"We will find out who did this, Mrs. Vincent. I promise."

Raquel nodded in response to Detective Garner's impassioned words.

They all knew who did this. It was Alexander's mistress. They just didn't know *which* one, and that hurt the most. Alexander was so careless and selfish. He constantly lied, cheated with more than one woman, and got himself killed.

"Raquel, we can go to the hotel now. There's no reason for you to stay here," Patrice said softly.

When they discovered Alexander's body, Deaton made sure his wife came to help comfort, Raquel. She'd had to lean on Patrice more in the last few months than she had in their entire twenty-year friendship. Patrice never complained and was there whenever she needed her without question. Raquel was more than thankful for her friend.

"Y—yes...yes, let's go. I need to leave this house." Raquel responded robotically.

In a blink of an eye, Raquel was riding in an elevator at the W Hotel. She didn't remember the car ride or checking into the hotel. She was a walking zombie. Moving through life with a cloudy disposition, she could only pray it was temporary.

"Wait here, Rocky. I'll run you a bath so you can relax." Noah's deep voice was colored with concern.

Raquel felt terrible that he even had to go through this with her. It wasn't fair for Noah to have to deal with the aftermath of her husband's poor choices. Noah was a victim of circumstance just as much as she was. And he shouldn't be responsible to help pick up the pieces of her broken life. Raquel stripped out of her clothes and with Noah's help, she carefully removed her boot. She slipped into the tub and closed her eyes. It wasn't long before she felt Noah's arms wrapped around her from behind. Noah had silently slipped into the tub and without any unnecessary words, as he comforted her with only his presence.

Raquel knew she was selfish for taking all of his strength and support without giving any in return. She knew she should tell him to leave and mean it. She knew she was wrong for loving a man who wasn't her dead husband because he had given her more love and compassion in a few months than Alexander had in the entirety of their marriage. Raquel felt guilty and ashamed of herself for wanting Noah, for needing him, for not wanting to ever let him go.

"I'm sorry," Raquel whispered.

"Why are *you*, sorry?" Noah questioned as he hugged her closer to his muscular chest.

"For keeping you here with me." Raquel's head lowered in humiliation.

"Hey." Noah pulled Raquel awkwardly onto his lap. She was able to look into his deep-set blue eyes as he spoke to her with conviction. "Nobody can keep me anywhere I don't want to be. I've already told you I'm not going anywhere." He leaned down and softly kissed her lips as they settled back into companionable silence.

Raquel didn't know how long they sat in the tub both lost in their thoughts, but by the time they got out and dried off, her fingers were wrinkled. Once dry, they slipped into bed without bothering with pajamas.

They gravitated toward each other, and Raquel was once again wrapped in Noah's strong arms. Both lay awake, neither speaking of their deceitful spouses. So many things could've been avoided if they would've just been honest.

Now, as Raquel lay awake, she wasn't sure if Giselle or Jana Strauss killed Alexander. She had no idea why either of the women would want to kill him or if they were going to target her next. Raquel was stressed the hell out, but she was finally able to drift off into a fitful sleep.

It seemed Raquel had only been asleep a few minutes when she woke up covered in sweat and breathing hard. The nightmare lingered on the verge of her consciousness, but for the life of her, she couldn't remember what had her so afraid.

Raquel slowly got out of bed and moved carefully to the bathroom. She splashed her face with cold water and tried to regulate her breathing. It took several minutes, but she was finally able to calm down. She didn't want to wake Noah, so instead of getting back in bed, she made her way to the large sitting area of the room.

Before she knew it, the sun was shining brightly through the sheer curtains when she felt butterfly kisses, pressing softly against her cheeks. She couldn't help the smile that graced her face as she looked into the beautiful, sapphire gaze.

"What are you doing out here? I missed you lying next to me." Noah whispered in Raquel's ear between showering her face with kisses.

"Mmmm..." Raquel moaned. "I couldn't sleep, so I came in here. I guess I dozed off."

"Well, I ordered breakfast. I'm going to hop in the shower before they get here. Would you like to join me?" Noah wiggled his eyebrows as he licked his lips, and Raquel chuckled.

She was so happy he was here, distracting her from her life. He was such a good man.

"No. I'll wait for room service to get here." She responded, still smiling.

"Suit yourself. I'll be out in a jiffy." Noah kissed her forehead before sauntering off to the bathroom.

Soon after, there was a knock on the door. Raquel was glad she didn't have to wait long for food because she just realized how hungry she was. As she limped slowly to the door, there was a more urgent knock.

"Coming!" Raquel yelled with a scowl. "They won't get a tip if they keep beating on the freaking door."

Raquel finally made it to the door after what seemed like ten minutes and flung it open. "Sorry about that, as you can see I can't move very fast." She started to smile, but it quickly faded when she realized she was staring down the barrel of a gun.

20

LOVE LIES

Noah got out of the shower. He had held Raquel through most of the night, and to feel her trembling body as she cried in her sleep broke his heart. Even though Alexander was the world's biggest prick, Noah understood why Raquel was so emotional. There was only so much one person could take, and although she held strong while awake, she couldn't control her emotions while she slept.

Noah wiped his hand across the foggy mirror, and his reflection revealed a man who was in dire need of a shave and haircut. His blond hair hung carelessly into his face, and the five o'clock shadow was now a beard. He ran his hand over his hairy chin and sighed. Raquel's life wasn't the only one in shambles. It was a reason Noah focused so intently on helping Raquel. It was so he wouldn't have to face his problems. Like Raquel's, his marriage was over. He should have been trying to pick up the pieces of a broken love, but all he could do was think of his future and where he stood with Raquel.

Noah knew he should've felt guilty for wanting Raquel so soon after she was made a widow. Hell, he wanted her before the bastard died. He couldn't even feel the least bit sad about Alexander's murder.

He wasn't the judgmental type, but there was only so much dirt one person could do before karma caught up.

Raquel was a beautiful person inside and out, and Alexander cheated on her with her boss of all people. There was something to be said about a man with that much audacity. But in the end, it caught up with him in the worst way possible.

The only thing Noah couldn't figure out was if Giselle was the person who pulled the trigger. Noah never considered his wife could be capable of such a heinous act. Yes, she was selfish and uncaring, but Noah never thought she could be a murderer. However, whether she'd killed Alexander or not, Giselle's hands were dirty. It wasn't a coincidence that the platinum blond woman, who was connected to Giselle, had been seen in the hospital when someone poisoned Raquel.

If she didn't shoot Alexander, she most certainly tried to kill Raquel. Noah didn't have a clue who Giselle was anymore, and it knocked him off kilter. He was a man who prided himself on knowing the people around him, knowing what they needed and wanted before they had to ask. But it was no longer the case, and the fact was disconcerting.

Noah continued to brush his teeth, and slick his hair back away from his face as he thought about all the signs he missed that could've prevented the entire chaotic situation he now found himself in. But time travel wasn't possible, so he had to tell himself to let it go. He had to focus on the present, not the past.

Noah wrapped the towel around his waist as he heard Raquel call she was coming. He knew room service must be at the door, so he slipped on a robe before joining her in the sitting room of the hotel suite. However, when he cracked open the bathroom door, what he saw was shocking. Someone had a gun pointed in Raquel's face.

Noah's gun was in the bedroom, but he knew he didn't have time to get it. He had to react quickly to save Raquel's life. He rushed into the sitting room, snatching both women's attention. His hands were held up in a non-threating gesture. "You don't want to do that. Just put the gun down." The bass in Noah's voice was commanding.

"Of course, I want to do this. This bitch ruined my life!" she shouted angrily. "Alexander was never going to leave you. Even after all the shit you did to him!"

Noah could see Raquel's hands trembling as she held them up in the air. He wouldn't let her be hurt, not again. He'd promised himself.

"Listen, Jana. It is *Jana*, right? Go ahead and point the gun at me, alright." Noah's voice was still demanding, but he didn't want to scare the woman.

It was clear she was out of her mind. How could the mistress blame the wife because her husband wanted to stay? What kind of backward ass craziness was that?

Jana shook her head. "No. Alexander is dead. Even after your slutty ass got knocked up by him," she pointed the gun at Noah, "he still wanted you! You should be dead too! I cut those brakes, you should be dead!" She pointed the gun back at Raquel.

The crazed look in the woman's eyes worried Noah, so he eased toward her slowly.

He noticed Raquel slowly shuffling backward, but with her cast, she wouldn't be able to maneuver too quickly if she needed to get out of the woman's warpath. Noah had to get close enough to Raquel to shield her if the woman got a shot off.

"Alexander is dead because he was a cunt who couldn't keep his dick in his pants!" Noah shouted, gaining the insane woman's attention.

Her hazel eyes narrowed, and she shifted the gun back in his direction. It was precisely the reaction he'd wanted. "No! That's not true!" Jana shook her head frantically. "He loved me. She was the one who cheated first." Jana pointed the gun at Raquel again.

Noah inched closer to Jana without her realizing it. There was no way he could block Raquel, but maybe he could get the gun away from her before she could get a shot off.

"That's not true. Sorry to break it to you, sweetheart, but Alexander has been fuckin' my wife for as long as he's been fuckin' you. He had no intention of bein' with you." Noah spat harshly, successfully gaining Jana's wrath.

"Fuck you, hillbilly. Who the hell do you think you are?" Jana stepped in his direction.

Like a man on a mission, Noah made his move. He yelled at Raquel to get down as he grabbed for the gun. Wrestling a crazy person, even one smaller than him, was more of a task than he anticipated. Noah pushed at Jana, but she pulled with all her might until...

Pow!

౷ఌఠ

THE GUNSHOT, WHICH HIT THE WALL, REVERBERATED LOUDLY around the suite. Then suddenly, Noah fell backward with Jana's body against his. As they hit the floor with a resounding thud. Noah's grip on the gun loosened and it slid across the floor. His ears rang, and the wind was knocked out of him. However, he didn't have time to catch his breath because Jana was going for the gun.

Noah grabbed her legs and tugged as hard as he could. The crazed woman kicked out, trying to dislodge Noah's grip. But he used his superior strength to hold her down. Noah subdued the woman as Raquel scurried over and retrieved the gun.

"Get the fuck off of me!" Jana screamed, bucking her body to remove Noah.

"Shut the hell up!" Noah was tired of dealing with deranged people. His patience was more than thin. It was now nonexistent.

"Call the police!" Noah shouted at Raquel as he pinned Jana's arms behind her back.

He didn't have to restrain Jana for long because hotel security was alerted about the gunshot. The men were able to cuff Jana and securely hold her until the police got there.

Noah sat impatiently as Raquel once again, answered questions.

"So, your boss pulled a gun on you because she killed your husband? After, she tried to kill you?" The uniformed officer asked.

"Yes. She said I ruined her life because Alexander didn't want a divorce. She apparently cut my brakes so that I would die and she could have him to herself."

All Noah could do was shake his head in astonishment. Jana Strauss was a lunatic and a gullible one at that. She believed every word

Alexander ever told her. Evidently, he had met the woman at a school function he'd attended with Raquel.

Alexander fed her every lie a cheating husband could tell his mistress. He'd claimed Raquel didn't show him any love or affection and she was cheating on him. Raquel was a bitch who degraded him every chance she got.

It was amazing how an educated woman such as Jana Strauss could take her own wrong-doings and completely place the blame on someone else.

"That will be enough questions for now, Officer Lambert. We'll take it from here." Detectives Garner and Witt finally arrived to take control of the scene.

Noah was glad the two had shown up because he was seconds away from punching Officer Lambert in the throat. He was the same idiot who barged into Raquel's hospital room to tell her Alexander had been reported missing. The only reason why Noah even let the man get close enough to Raquel was because he'd apologized profusely about his uncouth behavior.

According to Witt, Lambert was entirely too eager to jump on a high profile case, but he was harmless. That didn't stop Noah's irritation brought on by the officer's presence, though.

Soon, the suite was cleared of everyone except the crime scene photographers, Detectives Garner and Witt, Noah, and Raquel. The detectives had already taken Jana into custody, and she was being booked on both murder and attempted murder.

"Even though she confessed to cutting your brakes, we still don't have a connection from Ms. Strauss to your poisoning, Mrs. Vincent." Detective Garner told Raquel.

"Detective, just call me Raquel please." Noah was aware calling Raquel, Mrs. Vincent was bringing up the memory of Alexander's death.

"Okay, Raquel. Ms. Strauss was at your school's Math and Science night with a cafeteria full of parents and staff. She didn't leave the campus until around eight-thirty that evening. She didn't have time to go to the hospital and poison you."

"I know Strauss wasn't behind the poisoning," Noah spoke up. "Because Giselle was behind Raquel's poisoning."

"Why would you think your wife had something to do with Raquel's poisoning? You claimed she was behind the brakes, and we found out that wasn't the case." Detective Witt let his doubt in Noah show.

Noah didn't care if the detective believed him or not. This time he had proof.

"I have the security feed from the night of the poisoning." Noah retrieved his computer and pulled up the illegal feed.

"This woman," Noah pointed at the screen, "was with my wife at a hotel a few weeks ago." He refused to reveal how he'd gotten access to the security feed, but once the detectives saw the video for themselves, they weren't too caught up on Noah's secret resources.

"What hotel and what date? Maybe we can catch a break and get more security footage to prove your theory."

"It's not a theory. It's a fact." Noah stated in exasperation.

"It's not a fact until we get proof. We can't arrest your wife on your word alone." Detective Garner responded.

Noah nodded. He knew they would need proof of Giselle's involvement, so he would have to go back to Austin and set the bait. He knew how Giselle operated. Alexander had been her go-to, and now he was dead. So Noah knew she'd be back.

"I know how to get your proof."

GISELLE

"How in the hell did you talk me into this shit?" Aundrea questioned she was behaving like the anxious teenager she'd once been. Giselle didn't have time for Aundrea to fall apart, they were in deep shit, and they needed to keep their stories together.

"Money. Let's not pretend why you did this. But you have to keep it together. Stay out of sight and don't leave this hotel. I have a way to get us some money, and we can disappear." Giselle hoped her words sounded convincing because she was lying through her perfect white teeth.

Giselle had no intentions of taking Aundrea with her, once she got what she came to Austin for, she was getting on a plane to the nearest island that didn't have extradition laws.

"Fine. We can disappear with the money you get. But don't try to fuck me, Giselle. I'm not the same young girl that I was before." Aundrea's warning was gone unnoticed by Giselle.

Nobody was getting in the way of her living rich and free. Nobody.

۞

IT SEEMED LIKE FOREVER SINCE NOAH HAD BEEN IN HIS OWN HOME back in Austin. In the week since his return, Noah was able to secure information he would've never suspected. First of all, the woman with the platinum blond hair was Aundrea Parish; a hacker from Fort Worth, Texas. The woman was a recently released prison inmate.

Apparently, the woman and Giselle went back a long way. They spent time in juvie together when they were teenagers. Hustling men and writing fraudulent checks was their motivation back then. However, when they eventually got caught, instead of taking a deal, they did their time. Once they were released, they went their separate ways, and from what Noah could tell, they'd just reconnected about ten months ago.

Noah had no idea about Giselle's criminal record or that she was even capable of committing such atrocities, but obviously, she was still connected to her dark past and willing to continue to hurt people for her own gain.

Giselle was more conniving than Noah had given her credit for, and using Aundrea was smart. According to the information Noah acquired, Aundrea was quite sharp, and once he and Manny broke the firewall, he figured out she was the one who blocked him from gaining access to information about Alexander as well as Giselle's past.

However, once the firewall was breached, the information started pouring in. The sealed juvenile records were deeply buried, but after some intense digging, Noah found them. He also figured out why a woman who Giselle hadn't seen in years would be willing to help kill someone. They had done it before.

Technically, it was never proven that they'd killed Aundrea's stepfather. However, the details surrounding his death were suspicious, and the two teenagers had been suspects. They were the only ones who'd been close enough to the victim to give him the poison. It was suspected that the stepfather was abusive, but that was never proven either. It was a lot of circumstantial evidence, which didn't stick, so the authorities ended up dropping the case.

Giselle had gotten away with murder once, so Noah couldn't let her get away with trying to kill Raquel. It was time for her to pay for her crimes.

The sound of heels clicking against expensive floor tiles brought Noah out of his thoughts. He knew it was show time, and he just hoped the plan would work.

21

APOLOGIES AND ALIBIS

"Noah, I can't say it's good to see you." Giselle was smug as she sat down in the chair beside her estranged husband. She crossed her legs seductively and licked her lips. It was truly remarkable how arrogant Giselle actually was to believe her little display would entice Noah.

As usual, she was dressed overtly sexy. Her short, body-hugging lavender dress showed her petite frame. Her hair and makeup were done to perfection. She reminded Noah of some Hollywood actress.

Even with the familiar way she dressed and acted, Noah could still recognize the changes in Giselle. She was no longer wearing the mask she usually put on for him. Gone was the silly cheerleader façade she often displayed for Noah's benefit. In its place was a highly functioning sociopath.

"Giselle, stop the bullshit. You know why we're here." Noah cut to the chase. The less time spent in her presence, the better because he wasn't sure how long he could keep his composure.

Giselle sighed dramatically as she went into her expensive bag and retrieved the paperwork. "Here. You and I both know I deserve more than what you're trying to give me."

"You don't deserve shit from me! But I hope you get everything that's coming to you!" Noah's loud voice carried throughout the open space.

Giselle blanched at his harsh tone, but Noah didn't care. He just wanted to get what he'd come for and get away from his soon to be ex. She was poisonous to everyone she came across. Noah was just shocked it had taken him so long to see her for who she really was.

Noah angrily snatched the papers from Giselle's hands and quickly scanned them. She had agreed to sign the divorce papers, but only after Noah told her she would get a lump sum settlement. She wasn't entitled to anything because of the infidelity clause in their prenup, but it was the only way Noah could get her to meet with him face to face.

"Now, now, don't be so angry, big guy." Giselle chastised after regaining her composure. "The money you're giving me won't even put a dent in those deep pockets of yours," Giselle smirked again, showing her callousness.

"I just want to know why you did this, Giselle." Noah knew what he was doing by asking her the question. Just like in the past, Giselle wouldn't be able to resist telling him of her latest conquest.

Giselle shrugged her narrow shoulders absently. "Alexander was adventurous and willing to do things you never would've thought of. He just lacked a little money, but that was only temporary."

"Why was it temporary? Because he was willing to kill his wife for money?" The frown smeared across Noah's face, his blue eyes glinted with anger. He was disgusted with her nonchalant attitude about taking someone's life.

Giselle's smirk turned into a scowl. "Your precious Raquel was in the way. She deserved every..." Giselle stopped midsentence before taking a deep breath and regaining her composure.

Noah thought she was about to tell on herself, but it would've been too easy. "Nobody deserves to die because their spouse is a lying, cheating scumbag. I mean you didn't try to kill me for my money. Why is that?" Noah slid forward in his seat.

The thought had crossed his mind more than once. He wondered why she hadn't tried to take him out. Giselle would've inherited all of his money.

"I didn't try to kill anyone. And I can't control what men would do to be with me. Alexander was behind Raquel's car accident, and I had nothing to do with any of that. I wasn't the one who put her in the hospital. Her husband did that."

"Her husband, huh? So you had nothing to do with trying to kill Raquel? It was all Alexander?" Noah questioned.

"Of course, it was him. As I said, I didn't try to kill *anyone*." Giselle snapped.

"But you've killed in the past, so why not now?"

The shock on Giselle's face at Noah's words were priceless. She may not have been caught, but they both knew she was capable of murder. "I-I... I don't know what... what you're talking about." She stuttered nervously shifting in her seat.

"Sure, you do. Walter Parish. That was the man you helped kill. You used poison to be exact."

Giselle's eyes went wide, and she began to gather up her things. "I'm not going to sit here and let you accuse me of anything."

"They arrested Aundrea ten minutes ago, by the way. She was staying in a hotel room *you* rented. How long do you think it will take her to roll on you? Do you think she's going to stay quiet with all the evidence they have against her?" It was Noah's turn to wear the smug grin.

Giselle plopped down in her chair, her bravado leaving instantly. "I'm sorry, Noah. But I didn't try to kill Raquel. I wasn't even in Dallas. After the accident, Alexander couldn't finish what he started. He told me he was staying with Raquel because she was pregnant. He didn't want anything to do with me." Giselle's alligator tears rolled down her rosy cheeks.

Noah looked on in sickened disbelief. The audacity it took for Giselle to believe her tears would still affect him after everything she'd put him through.

"So why was your friend the one on the video footage poisoning Raquel?" Noah questioned his words laced with disapproval.

"I don't know. I wasn't there! I swear, Noah. Please believe me." Giselle's tears came faster as she pleaded with Noah.

Noah shook his head. He couldn't believe she was sticking to her story. It didn't matter what she said, he knew she had everything to do with Raquel being poisoned, and so did the police.

"You're a liar, and I can't believe a single word that comes out of your mouth, including your fucked up apology. You tried to kill Raquel and succeeded in killing her baby, *my* baby. So fuck your tears!" Noah got up from the table as the police swarmed the area.

His wire may not have gotten the confession of murder, but Giselle unknowingly confessed to conspiracy to commit a crime. She knew about Alexander's plan to hurt Raquel, yet she'd done nothing to stop it nor did she contact the authorities. Giselle was going to be locked up whether she liked it or not, and there wasn't shit she could do about it.

Of course, it wasn't the outcome Noah wanted, but at least it was a start. Giselle would be in prison, and he would be free because she'd signed the divorce papers.

※

It had been three months since Raquel had laid eyes on Noah. *Three whole months* since Giselle was sentenced to twenty-five-years prison. It turned out that Aundrea Parish wasn't such a pushover after all. Giselle thought Aundrea wouldn't turn on her, and she thought their bond was still as solid as it was when they were teenagers. However, Aundrea was not the same naïve girl who'd done time out of loyalty. She had done real prison time, and she refused to go down alone.

So when Aundrea was presented with video evidence of her in the hospital, she sang like Whitney at the Super Bowl. Aundrea told any and everything she knew about Giselle and was smart enough to have voice recordings as proof. The reason behind everything was simple for Aundrea. *Money.* As a felon, Aundrea wanted fast money and a *lot* of it.

It was merely a coincidence when Aundrea ran into Giselle while she was sneaking around with Alexander in Dallas. Giselle and Alexander convinced Aundrea that getting rid of Raquel would be easy, and nobody would connect her back to either one of them since their juvenile records were sealed.

Aundrea had initially agreed to help them cover their tracks and block Alexander's records. When the couple paid her quickly, and then asked for another favor, she went along with their elaborate plan to kill Raquel.

When Raquel survived the car accident, they needed another way to get rid of her in order for Alexander to cash in on the million-dollar insurance policy he had on her. Aundrea was desperate for the money so she went with poison.

But when it was all said and done, even with her plea deal, Aundrea still received ten years in prison, and Raquel was satisfied with that.

After the trial was over, Noah went back to Austin, and Raquel stayed in Dallas trying to pick up the pieces of her mangled life. Although they spoke on the phone quite often, Raquel hadn't seen Noah, and she could admit she missed him tremendously. She missed the stability he provided and the love and care he showed her without hesitation.

After finding out all the details in Giselle's trial, Raquel was even more of a train wreck. Giselle had known all along about Alexander's affair with Jana. They were going to use her as another pawn in their diabolical schemes, but they found out too late that Jana was so unpredictable, so they brought in Aundrea. But Jana refused to go away.

They had a plan to set Jana up for Raquel's murder, but the crazed woman killed Alexander before they could put their plan into action.

After Jana was sentenced to life for Alexander's death, Raquel retreated into herself. She began to feel guilt over all of the loss of life that surrounded her.

It all seemed so senseless, and it could've been prevented. However, the choices other people made were not her fault. She was learning how to cope with everything and she continued to see Dr. Oliver two times a week.

Raquel decided to take an indefinite leave of absence from her job, and she even sold her house. The memories and betrayal were too much for her to bear, so starting over was the right thing to do.

"I like this place. It suits you." Patrice looked around the spacious ranch style home Raquel purchased in the outskirts of Dallas.

Raquel wanted to get away from the city for a while, but she wasn't equipped to move too far from her best friend. Patrice was the only family she had, and it would've been too traumatic for Raquel to just up and leave altogether.

"Thanks, I really loved it when I first saw it. And the plus side is it's still only twenty minutes from you guys." Raquel gave Patrice a genuine smile as she continued to unpack her kitchen.

"Well, I'm extremely proud of you. I always knew you were strong. But *geez*, I didn't realize just how strong. You could've let any of the things you went through break you." Patrice shook her head in awe. "But you kept on pushing. I can honestly say I don't know if I would've made it through all of that."

Raquel walked around the large kitchen island and embraced her best friend. "Listen, if it weren't for you and Deaton, I don't think I would've made it either. I know I've said this before, but I appreciate ya'll so much."

The women stood hugging each other and fighting back the tears that threatened to fall. They'd been through so much together, and Raquel would be eternally grateful for the love and support Patrice and Deaton had given her.

"Okay, let's get back to work and stop all this blubbering. You know my OCD won't allow me to sleep without this being finished." Raquel chuckled as she wiped her tears away.

Patrice laughed as she wiped her own tears, and they got back to work. It had only been a few minutes when to Raquel's surprise, the doorbell rang. Deaton was at work, and the only other person who knew her address was Patrice.

"I wonder who that could be?" Raquel questioned out loud.

"Probably Amazon. You know how you are." Patrice chuckled, and Raquel had to laugh because her purchases alone could probably keep Amazon in business.

Raquel looked through the peephole and was shocked to see who it was. "Noah!" She rushed him and slung her arms around his neck.

"Hey, Rocky. Miss me?" He gave her a sexy smile.

Raquel's heartbeat increased tenfold. "Yes, I missed you. Where the hell have you been?" Raquel demanded to know.

"Just getting my shit together."

"Whatever that means." Raquel smiled because if she knew anything about Noah Palmer, it was he did things in his own time. "Come on in. You can help me unpack."

Raquel was ecstatic to see Noah. It was like a missing piece of her had returned. Although she missed him, she was glad they were able to spend the time apart. Raquel was well aware of her dependency on him. And although she still had a lot of issues, with counseling she was much better equipped to handle them.

"Aren't you going to ask me why I'm here?" Noah asked as he trailed her into the house.

"No." Raquel shook her head. "It doesn't matter why. I'm just happy to see you." She gave him a bright smile, which he returned.

"That's good to know. I'm happy to see you too and I promise we'll never go that long without seeing each other again." Before she could blink, Noah pulled Raquel into his strong arms, and she instantly melted against him just like she did the very first time.

EPILOGUE

BEGIN AGAIN

TWO YEARS LATER...

Raquel felt the familiar calloused hands as they skimmed across her hypersensitive skin. His fingers pinched and tugged on the hardened nubs until pleasure filled her core. Raquel was now well acquainted with the feeling of butterflies fluttering wildly in her belly every time Noah touched her. Her breathing was labored with every provocative touch of his sinful fingers.

"Baby, please, I can't take anymore! Please! You know what you do to me." Raquel moaned out in pleasure when Noah continued to play her body masterfully. His touch was driving her to the brink of insanity.

"Shhhh. No begging, you know the rules, I'll give you what you need." Noah's deep voice vibrated in her ear, reminding her of the very first time they were together. His voice had darkened as it always did when he was dominating her in bed.

"Noaaah, please stop teasing me!" Raquel whimpered breathlessly.

"Shhh. Hush. I know you can take it. Now, be a good girl and turn over." Noah directed.

Eagerly, Raquel did as he'd commanded. She was on her belly face down when she felt Noah tug her body up. She was on all fours and smiling wickedly because she knew what was coming. Smack! Raquel moaned once more at the hard slap against her round ass. He repeated the hard smacks on each cheek, aggressively squeezing and slapping her round globes until Raquel was wet and panting in bliss.

After he finished her spanking, Noah rubbed her ass tenderly and then kissed it before she felt the heat of his chest against her back. He slid his hands beneath her body and once again, stimulated her full breasts and nipples. Raquel could feel his hard cock pressed against her ass, and she was more than ready for him to plunge his massive dick into her waiting core.

"Noooah," Raquel whined as she wiggled her ass in the air. Noah had the nerve to chuckle in response, and she had to look over her shoulder to glare at him.

"It's okay, Rocky. Don't I always give you what you need?"

Before she could answer him, Noah thrust deep inside her silky folds. They both groaned out their pleasure. Noah didn't wait for her to adjust to his size. He began rocking in and out of her like a man possessed.

"You feel so good, baby. Fuck, Rocky!" Noah growled in Raquel's ear.

"Oh, yes! That's it, babe, right there! Yesss!" Raquel squealed out in ecstasy.

Noah grunted as he lifted off her back. He smacked her ass again just the way she liked it and then he reached around and rubbed her pleasure button.

Raquel rocked her hips, smashing her clit against his finger. Noah increased the pressure and Raquel thought she'd died and gone to heaven. Pleasure coursed hot and heavy through her veins. The orgasm started in the tips of her toes and radiated outward engulfing her entire existence.

No one else on earth could make Raquel feel the way he did. Even after everything they'd been through, he was the only man who could love her completely.

Noah and Raquel gave and received pleasure to one another as they made love all night long. They basked in their passion, not wanting to be anywhere else in the world.

⚜

"THIS IS SUCH A BEAUTIFUL VIEW. JUST LOOK AT THAT WATER." Raquel sighed as Noah wrapped his strong arms around her from behind.

"Yeah, and you better take it all in and enjoy it, Rocky because we only have two days left before it's back to reality." Noah leaned down and kissed his wife on her head.

Noah heard Raquel sigh again loudly. "Do we *have* to go back? I mean can't we just stay here for the rest of our lives? Maybe become beach bums or something?"

Noah chuckled. "I don't think Patrice and Deaton would appreciate having to raise our kids because we decided to become beach bums."

Raquel giggled. "Oh please believe Auntie Patrice would be on a plane with our sweet angels so fast that our heads would spin."

Noah laughed along with his wife. Their two boys were a year apart at one and two, and they were very precocious and sometimes, mischievous. They were rambunctious boys who weren't afraid to get dirty, ask questions, and cause a little trouble. They were Noah and Raquel's pride and joy.

The day Noah showed up on Raquel's doorstep was also the day his divorce was finalized. He had spent the entire three months transferring and finding suitable accommodations for his business in Dallas. Noah had been in lust with Raquel from the beginning, but with everything they'd gone through together, he had completely fallen in love with her.

Moving back to Austin and away from Raquel was entirely out of the question. He would never be able to live without her. So instead of pretending he could, he made all the necessary efforts to keep her in his life.

He would forever be thankful for the time spent at Diamond's Resort where he met Raquel, but the only *open* thing in their relationship was communication. They were open-minded people and would never knock or judge anyone for what they wanted to do, but they decided without hesitation, swinging wasn't for them.

"I love you so much." Raquel's onyx eyes held him captive. Noah would never be used to the effect she had on him.

He leaned down and kissed her lips softly. "And I love you, Rocky."

"What do you say we strip down and take a little swim in the pool?" Raquel wiggled her voluptuous ass with mischief dancing in her eyes.

Noah laughed as he stripped off his shorts. "Last one there is a rotten egg."

They may not have been swingers, but a little naughty naked time during the day in a private pool was definitely right up their alleys.

"You're so bad." Raquel giggled as she took off, running toward the pool.

"And you love me!" Noah yelled as he raced after her.

"More than anything in the world."

THE END.

Made in the USA
Middletown, DE
05 November 2022

14197564R00097